CALLED BY DRAGON'S SONG

RETURN OF THE DRAGONBORN BOOK 3

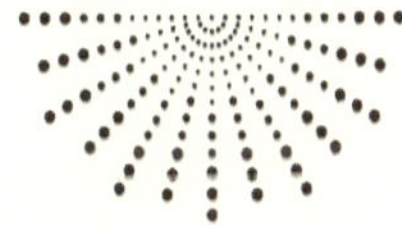

N.M. HOWELL

Written in collaboration with

H.F. STARK

Cover by

COVERS BY JUAN

DUNGEON MEDIA CORP.

This is a **work of fiction**. Names, characters, businesses, places, events, and incidents are either the products of the author's imagination or used in a fictitious manner. Any resemblance to actual persons, living or dead, or actual events is purely coincidental.

No part of this publication may be reproduced, stored in a retrieval system, or transmitted, in any form or in any means – by electronic, mechanical, photocopying, recording or otherwise – without prior written permission.

A dragon-sized thank you to J.
Without you, this story never would have seen
the light.
And thanks to Colin for your help in the inevitable
mad scramble toward the end.

PROLOGUE

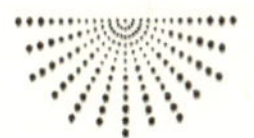

Six joyful yet trying months had passed since Chancellor Myamar Mharú and his enhanced battalion nearly wiped out Arvall. The city had since been in a state of complete overhaul after learning the truth about the dragonborn and slowly welcoming them. Elections were held and new leaders and officials put in office all over the region. Trials had taken place daily, resulting in a wide range of sentences and revealing just how evil and cruel the University had truly been.

The destruction to the city was unimaginable, and the escaped members of the Chancellor's battalion periodically set off bombs around the city to inspire fear. But things were slowly beginning to improve. Delegations comprised of both Arvall citizens and dragonborn ambassadors were sent out on regular diplomatic assignments to spread the truth about the dragonborn and win people to the cause. Arvall had spent millions of dollars in promoting tourism, inviting people to the city and the region to experience firsthand the magic and kindness of the dragonborn. Though some found it hard or impossible to stop a lifetime's worth of hatred, many hearts were changing. Thousands of hearts were changing. Perhaps even more.

The University was soon to be reopened. Lymir and his entire staff worked tirelessly since their appointments. They were making every effort to make the University a welcoming place to both magical and nonmagical people. New courses and professors were added, and while they've ensured that the University's cruelty will never be forgotten and that future generations will always be taught about the atrocities that the University committed, all courses propagating hate of the dragonborn and dragons were removed. The damage to the building was repaired and the halls were alive with excitement and comradery. The hideous murals celebrating the bloodbath of the dragonborn slaughter had been removed and a new mural celebrating the feats and power of the dragonborn had been painted.

Most promising of all was the integration of the dragonborn into modern society. Since the revelation of the University's lies, the citizens of Arvall had gone out of their way to make the dragonborn feel safe and welcome. Though the home of the dragonborn was still in the Hot Salts of Mithraldia, they frequently came down and sojourned among the citizens to learn and grow. Many dragonborn live temporarily in the caves along Brie Mountain. The citizens have also learned a tremendous amount of knowledge and wisdom from the dragonborn. There had been skirmishes when visitors balked at the idea of the dragonborn coexisting in the modern world; several small factions from other parts of Noelle had come to Arvall City to attack or otherwise provoke the dragonborn and prove that they truly are evil. Yet, for the first time in nearly a thousand years, dragons and dragonborn lived among everyone else and could do so freely. Happily.

It was widely known as "The Great Peace," the first time in the history of Noelle that so many cities and regions have ceased competition and came under one banner of understanding.

CHAPTER ONE

A BATTALION SOLDIER HELD HIM UNDER EITHER ARM as Ashur took his first steps since that fateful night six months prior. He grew furious with each step, knowing that the soldiers at his sides were doing most of the work, but he could barely hold his own head. His legs felt like lead weights and the pain was indescribable. He only had the strength not to scream; the last thing he could afford was to look even weaker. The battalion was incredibly loyal to him, but he didn't want to test that. It had already been months since they'd had a decent meal, shelter fit for human beings, and even longer since they'd been able to lead normal lives.

"Great work, my leader," a soldier said. "You'll be doing this unaided soon."

"Yes, very admirable, my leader," said another.

Their praise made Ashur angrier because he knew they were lying. He shoved them both off and fell to the ground. They tried to pick him up, but he held up his hand to stop them. Then he began the slow process of standing up, which he hadn't done in months. The pain was agonizing and his head ached so much he thought it might split. His arms and legs shook under the strain of trying to raise himself and already he sweated heavily. But, one thing he could not allow himself to do was quit. He focused his mind, drawing a picture to himself of his goal, his most desperate desire. He let that picture fuel his body. He pushed himself up and with a final furious heave, he stood on his legs by his own power.

"Incredible!" someone said. "The doc said he wouldn't be able to stand on his own for weeks!"

"No doctor has a clue what our leader is capable of," said Lucas. "He is the future."

The battalion saluted Ashur as he trembled on his feet. He felt some small amount of pride return to him as he balanced there, thinking that this weakened state was not him, but Tarven. It reminded him of who and what he used to be. But he focused again, envisioning the picture in his mind that had driven him since he first opened his eyes on the operating table. A field covered in the bloody corpses of the dragonborn, Andie Rogers' head in his hand.

ANDIE STOOD in the May Cave, high in the mountains in the Hot Salts of Mithraldia. The day of the ceremony finally arrived and she was more nervous than she thought she'd be. She lived among her own people for a while, but still felt like an outsider. They had welcomed her with open arms, but their experiences had been so different she still found it hard to relate to them sometimes. That aside, she felt more at home than ever. She opened herself to every aspect of their way of life and she learned and grew so much among them. On this day they honored her, again, for her actions the night of the confrontation in Arvall, which most of Noelle now called the "Night of Revelation." All she knew about the ceremony was that the dragonborn presented her with a very great, very precious gift. Apparently, it was extremely rare and an honor of the highest degree. As Andie stood, waiting, she saw Saeryn coming toward her.

"Saeryn," Andie called, giving a low bow.

"Princess Andie," Saeryn responded with a smile.

They hugged and Saeryn led Andie through the crowd, toward the center of the cave where a dais had been set up.

"I'm sure you must have a lot of questions," Saeryn said.

"I always have questions about everything the

dragonborn do, but what I'm really wondering is why I'm being honored... again."

"I know it must seem a bit... overzealous of us, but you quite literally saved our lives, Andie. Again. There's no amount of gifts or honors or ceremonies that could repay that debt, though I assure you this is the last. At least until you save our lives again. The dragonborn are a respectful and thankful people. Admittedly, we do tend to overexert ourselves in our gratefulness. But I want you to know that no matter how uncomfortable you feel and no matter what you may think of the ceremony or your own worth, you have earned this honor. It is rightfully yours and you should embrace it."

"I'll do my best. To be honest, I wish I could honor you and our people. You're telling me about unpayable debts, but you and the dragonborn have finally given me a home, finally made me feel like I belong. For years I lived in fear, in a world that hated me and would have executed me if they knew what I was. When you and our people came, you saved me. So as far as incredible debts go, I think we're even."

The two of them arrived at the dais just as the elders did. All around them were the dragonborn who gathered with smiles of joy to see their princess honored. Many had come back from Arvall just for this occasion. A buzz of expectation and low chatter hung over the setting. While she waited, Andie glanced around the cave.

When a person heard of the dragonborn living in a cave, their first reaction is bafflement. No one understood how a people as powerful and beautiful as the dragonborn could allow themselves to live in caves. But the caves were just the beginning. Not only do the dragonborn spend countless hours making perfect networks of tunnels, they also improved the caves; it wasn't quite decorating, but a dragonborn cave was no dank, dark cubby.

The dragonborn used their magic and traditions to smooth and shape the walls, level the floors, and purify the air. They spent countless days casting spells against cold, sickness, insects, weak foundation, and more. The dragonborn were also gifted craftsmen and artisans, and could make the most beautiful fixtures, ornaments, and furniture. One of the greatest tools they had was the fire of their dragons. They brought the dragons into the caves and had them breathe fire against the walls while they cast magic at the same time. They called it "waking," literally bringing the cave to life. Waking left the cave walls pearlescent and color-changing. The first time Andie saw it she nearly cried from the beauty.

The May Cave was the central cave, the largest and highest in the network, and the only cave that could hold all of the dragonborn at once. It was used for ceremonies, meetings, and other important events. Andie gazed at its shimmering walls and perfectly smooth surfaces. Its absolutely clear air and the brilliant, yet soft light that emanated from the walls. It seemed a crime to call it a cave.

"I believe we're all here," Saeryn said. "Perhaps we should get started."

Silence followed her voice as if she had released a command. Every eye looked up at the Queen, who looked as beautiful and regal as ever. Saeryn turned to Andie and gestured for her to join her at the front of the dais. Andie went over, nervous. A vigorous applause sounded as she took her place beside the Queen.

"We have gathered this afternoon to pay homage, yet again, to our princess and hero, Andryne Rogers. She's lived among us for a while now and I believe I speak for every soul here when I say we are proud and humbled to have her. Today the elders and I would like to bestow a gift, one of the rarest and most powerful we could ever give. This is one of our most sacred and heartfelt gifts. Elders, if you will."

The elders moved forward, carrying a chest between them. Regardless of their age, they seemed to handle the large chest with minimal effort. They sat it down beside the feet of the Queen and opened it. They lifted the gift out and held it. Andie couldn't take her eyes off it. A collective gasp made its way through the cave.

"Yes, it is quite extraordinary, if I do say so myself. Such beauty." Saeryn's voice echoed through the cave, overwhelming the silence that fell upon the room. "This is the Aethrailaer. Armor that has not been seen or made in many centuries. This kind of armor is made by taking a few scales from every living dragon and combining them on a gold and iron frame. Only scales that have naturally fallen can be used. As you can imagine, in the old times all the dragons were hardly ever in the same place and scales disintegrate so easily if they are not quickly preserved. We started on this as soon as we landed in the Hot Salts after leaving the portal and now it's finally ready. Andryne, this is from all of us."

The elders presented the armor to Andie. She reached out to take it, her face a reflection of pure awe and joy. It was heavier than it looked. The scales had been tightly, seamlessly woven together over a golden frame. It was clearly magical craftmanship, unlike anything Andie had ever seen. The gold frame had been enchanted and was not only flexible, but also shimmered in response to Andie's touch. The scales themselves were the same beautiful, iridescent sheen as when they were on the dragons' backs. The working and design of the armor was flawless, the most exquisite she'd ever seen.

"Thank you for this," Andie whispered through a clenched throat. She was speechless. Tears threatened to spill from her lids as she stared down at the remarkable beauty of the armor. It took her a long moment to collect her thoughts enough to speak. "I know you all want to congratulate me and praise me for bringing peace to our world. And maybe I did. But I owe you just as much, and I plan to repay that debt by being worthy of this armor and never failing you. It'll be a dark day if I ever need this, but it's a beautiful and peerless gift. I'm going to display it near my office at the University. Thank you."

Everyone applauded. Andie did, too. She had never felt prouder. Saeryn hugged her again and then each of the ten elders shook her hand.

"Alright, everyone. I promised Andie this would be a brief, yet sincere ceremony and I believe we've thanked her enough for today. Thank you all for coming out and please go in peace."

The dragonborn gave their last smiles to Andie and drifted out of the room. The elders offered her some encouraging words and they left, too. Andie and Saeryn turned and descended the dais, heading into the tunnel that led out high onto the west side of the mountain. They came out into the open air. Dragons swooped above them and below was a field of clouds hiding the raging storms that ceaselessly plagued the region.

"Now that we're alone, we need to talk about Arvall," Andie said. "I just got another letter from Marcus. He said 'Fhealltóir Fola' is beginning to show up a lot more around the city and its outlying districts. The more they look into it, the less sure they are about who's really setting off these bombs. It might be the battalion or it might be the ancient enemy of our people. The Beautiful Dead. I think it's safe to assume that they're still around and still angry."

"Yes, it seems that for all our kindness and patient ways, we dragonborn cannot help making the worst enemies imaginable. Make no mistake, though the name of this group may sound attractive, there is nothing gentle in their methods. They are a darker enemy than anyone should have to face."

"Why do they call you blood traitors?"

"We share a common ancestor."

"Another ancient people?"

"Dragons. You see the University became so obsessed with rewriting history in order to eradicate our people that they left out the other half of our origin story. A second group of people were descended from the great dragons. The Beautiful Dead are actually somewhat older than us. When their people came into existence, they had no magic. They were incredibly strong, fast, agile. They had heightened senses and hunting abilities. While we obtained our magic from the dragons, the Beautiful

Dead acquired physical attributes. They are absolutely lethal.

"Then the dragonborn came along and were given the gift of magic. This drove our older brothers insane with jealousy. They didn't just want physical abilities, they wanted the power to cast spells as well. It wasn't long before they discovered that by drinking our blood they could obtain our magic. The Beautiful Dead are aggressive and belligerent by nature, and we knew that if they ever obtained our power there would be no stopping them. They would consume the world. So, we fought them. For centuries. It wasn't until my great grandfather came along that we finally defeated them. He was a powerful sorcerer and he devised a spell that would bind their blood, so that even if they drank from us they would never obtain our magic. And that spell is never-ending so long as the corresponding bloodline in our people is protected."

"Let me guess... that bloodline is ours?"

"I'm afraid so."

"Super."

"Whoever is left of our line must be protected at all costs."

"The whole blood traitor thing makes sense now. Looks like we have another battle on our hands. Fortunately, you and I have been studying the grimoires for months."

"And learned a considerable amount."

"So, there's the Beautiful Dead, the Battalion, and a host of other smaller threats, and we have no idea where any of them are or what they're planning. It's going to be a long year."

A messenger came running from the caves. He bowed and handed the letter to Saeryn. After reading it, Saeryn looked at Andie solemnly.

"It's another warning from your Professor Marcus," she said. "They're still finding bombs, though thankfully no more have gone off. He's also warning us that the city has been getting a lot of rather serious threats from eastern Noelle."

"Well, we always knew we had our work cut out for us," Andie said, gripping her armor tighter. "We'll deal with them as they come. Right now, we need to get ready to fly to Arvall. If we leave by dusk we can make it to the ceremony."

CHAPTER TWO

Andie, Saeryn, and Lymir stood with the rest of the faculty and staff of the University. The day had finally come to reopen the institution under its new mission.

Lymir stepped forward and began his speech, but Andie was too busy to listen. She and the other high members of the University had received an onslaught of angry, vengeful letters in the preceding days. Some had been mere reminders of how eastern Noelle felt, but others had been too evil to ignore. Precautions, both tactical and magical, had been taken to make sure that nothing happened on the first day. The police force of Arvall were also called to help keep the peace. Still, just that morning Andie received a letter demanding they close the school or risk being attacked. The letter threatened that the dragonborn and dragons would be eradicated for good. It was signed by the battalion.

Andie knew that wherever he was, Ashur was plotting his revenge. Saeryn thought it best not to tell the people about the letters. The other members agreed. They all believed it was high time they opened the University and set the world back on the right track. Enjoying the era of the Great Peace was just as important as protecting it.

"…which is what we've always wanted," Lymir said. "Finally, the citizens of the world have begun to welcome the dragonborn to live among them and to teach them. I believe the coming days will be the best the world has ever known. While it would be foolish to assume that we can change every heart, I know we can still make this world the place it always should have been and that starts today, with reopening of the University. Once a stark symbol of oppression and murder, this institution will now be dedicated to helping any and all who walk through its doors. We will educate…"

Andie couldn't leave her place on the podium, but she focused all of her attention on surveying the crowd and the area. She was almost certain this was a mistake; they'd risked all these lives and the reopening of the University just so they could show that they were strong. She wondered if that strength would be enough once the bombs began. But before she knew it the audience was clapping, Lymir was done, and the ribbon was cut. The ceremony was complete and confetti and balloons rained down.

Andie turned to Saeryn, who looked just as concerned as she was, and then motioned for them to leave. They smiled and waved to the crowd before hurrying off. Everyone else headed to the front doors to see the University. Oren found his way out of the crowd and over to them, with Lymir close on his heels.

"I can see you were just as anxious as I," Saeryn said to Andie. "I seriously doubted our decision."

"Yeah," Andie responded. "I was sure something awful was going to happen. And I still don't feel comfortable enough to feel safe."

"I have been extremely watchful all morning," Oren said. "I haven't been able to relax for a fortnight and today I seem more suspicious than ever. I don't care to have so many enemies about and to not know where they are or what they want to do."

"I think we're all a little anxious today," Lymir said. "And for good reasons. At least with the University we knew exactly who the enemy was, where they were located, and what they were capable of. We still don't understand the full extent of the battalion's armor or of how the Dead have adapted in the last centuries. And we've received threats from at least two hundred other smaller groups."

"Two hundred?" Saeryn asked.

"The danger is far from over. I still believe Arvall City and the Hot Salts are safe, but for how long? I think it might be best if we sent a party to investigate."

"I would second that," said Oren. "It's time we became more proactive. Our enemies won't dare to show their faces yet, but the more we let them get away with, the more they will attempt. I could lead a party out now."

"I'll go with you," Andie said. "And we can get a couple more dragonborn to fly with us. Saeryn and Lymir could get the Arvall police to increase patrols, at least for tonight. We could leave now and fly north. That seems to be where most of the letters are coming from and the field burnings are in the northern tracts of the String Fields."

"Be careful, princess," said Saeryn.

Saeryn and Lymir turned to search for the police, and Andie and Oren made their way to Oren's dragon. Andie still found herself disappointed that there was not a dragon for her yet, but she had been told to give it more time. She and Oren mounted the dragon and Oren signaled three nearby dragonborn. They all took off. Andie looked back and just before the people were too small to make out anymore, she saw him. Raesh.

· · ·

They flew north to Taline. They landed at the edge of the city and go on foot. Since the Chancellor and his men were stopped, Taline had finally experienced peace and been allowed the chance to get back on its feet. The city thrived with Stefan's leadership. Andie and Oren met with him to see what news he has.

"We've received some rather cruel sounding missives, but nothing like what you're getting in Arvall," Stefan said. "Honestly, things are quiet here. Without the bombings and destruction that Mharú subjected us to, the city was finally able to rest and come together. We have taken precautions, though. We've strengthened security along Gordric's Pain and set up watchtowers along the silver cliffs. We conduct weekly patrols as far south as Michaelson and as far North as the Church of Stone and Sea. We've tried our best to catch whoever is burning the messages into the String Fields, but they continue to elude us. If you're looking for my opinion on the matter, I agree with you. Whoever your enemies are, they lie to the north. I would suggest you visit the Church. I don't often go on patrols myself, but I happened to go on the last round. I wasn't at all satisfied with their behavior. The Church has always been... odd, but this was something else entirely. You could do worse than to investigate there."

· · ·

THEY LEFT Taline and flew all night and all morning until they reached the Church at dawn. Andie had heard many stories of the Church, but nothing could have prepared her for it. The Church of Stone and Sea was exactly what its name described. A sacred house of worship built from the red sand of the very beach on which it stood. Its foundation was made from the last of Noelle's Voldredarian stone—a material as hard as steel, more valuable than gold, and enchanted to sing persuasive hymns to all passersby. Many who stay too long around the Church never leave. The red sand made the Church one of the most beautiful buildings Andie had ever seen, perhaps the only structure that ever rivaled the dragonborn caves. But what was most impressive about this building was not its vermillion walls or even the songs of its stones. It was the sheer size of the structure. The Church was the largest manmade structure in history. It stood at over two hundred meters tall and was more than twenty kilometers long and as many wide. It took over a thousand years to build. Andie was speechless.

"I never knew men could make such things," Oren said.

"You and me both," Andie said, craning her neck. "You never came here before?"

"No. The Church was already completed by the time I grew of age, but the dragonborn have always stayed away from this place. One hears stories of terrible things. Our people believe this place isn't enchanted, but cursed."

"But it's a church. Right?"

"No, it is much more than that. Inside those walls is an entire culture. They are an entirely different race, completely self-sustaining. Many people who go in never see the light of day again. No one knows what happens to them. And the priests, if they can be called that, are said to be the most dangerous of all, hardly the holy men you might anticipate."

"What's so dangerous about them?"

"I've only heard stories and perhaps none of them were true, but be on guard here, princess. We don't know anything about these people. Can you hear it? The hymn?"

Andie turned her ear to the Church and focused; not only did she hear the hymn, she realized she had been hearing it since she landed. In fact, she even knew the words. The Church had been singing to her ever since she came into its range. Suddenly, she knew exactly what the Church wanted and what part she could play. What part she *should* play. Before she could hear anymore, Andie cast a spell to block the hymn. Instantly, she felt her autonomy and her own mind return.

Andie and the others walked toward the Church, entering its unbelievably massive shadow. The Church was the most beautiful and dazzling building she had ever seen, but without its hypnotic hymn in her ears, Andie was able to think clearly and stay focused. As they came to the gargantuan front doors, they opened without warning. It was a triple door. The two side doors swung slowly inward and the middle door swung inward and up. Oren and the others hesitated for a moment, but Andie beckoned them forward.

"It's unsettling, I know," she said. "But somebody seems to be expecting us. I don't know how I'm supposed to feel about that."

They entered and found themselves inside a cavernous foyer, totally alone. Once they cleared the path of the doors, the triple doors close behind them, completely soundless. Andie and Oren shared a look. Andie looked around and if it hadn't been for the knots in her stomach she might have been floored by the total, genius beauty of the place. The fixtures and furniture were expertly crafted in red and gold, gothic style, with the posts and points so sharp they could be daggers. Now that she was closer to the red sand walls, Andie could see that they were also reflective. She could see herself looking back. Right before her eyes, a line appeared in the wall.

The line, at first, looked like a split, but then it grew and began to separate the wall. As the split grew, the sand lost its fixed state and began to spill, but did so in a predesigned pattern, falling to the floor and running into two neat piles on either side of the new opening in the wall. Soon after, a perfect rectangular opening had appeared and six men moved toward Andie and her friends. The men were clad in translucent robes so that you can see their bodies beneath, but couldn't make out details. It unnerved Andie. The men's faces, however, were covered with the same red sand as the walls, leaving only a space for their mouths. Andie was incredibly tempted to ask them if they could see. Her curiosity was quickly replaced by a mix of wonder and dread as the men came to a stop just in front of her, forming a perfect line, side-by-side.

"Welcome..."

"Travelers..."

"To..."

"This..."

"Our..."

"Church."

Each man spoke one word and allowed the next to continue. Of all the things Andie had seen in the Church so far, this was by far the eeriest. For a moment neither she nor Oren could speak.

"And we thank you for your welcome," Oren finally said. "Might I be right in assuming you are the famous priests of the Church?"

"We..."

"Are..."

"But..."

"Six..."

"Of..."

"Them."

"I see. We ask your forgiveness for our intrusion here, but we are of the dragonborn people recently brought to your world from another time. What we seek is knowledge of our enemies, who seem to increase by the day. We have received a series of threats and—"

"Do..."

"You..."

"Charge..."

"Us..."

"With..."

"Machinations?"

"Certainly not. We're only here to inquire if you have heard anything that might help us gauge where our enemies are or what they might be up to. Many of the letters we've received seem to have come from your region. We accuse you of nothing, but we have heard of the admirable watch you keep over this region and its movements. Have you heard anything that might be of assistance to us?"

Oren waited for an answer, but the men simply stood there, facing straight ahead without moving or making a sound. Andie got the distinct impression that they were doing something deliberate that she and her friends couldn't see.

"Wise priests," Oren began again. "My comrades and I mean you no harm, nor do we wish to interfere with the workings of your Church. We ask nothing of you but information. Here with me today is someone very important to our people. This is Andie Rogers—"

"Don't..."

"Lie."

"It..."

"Surely..."

"Cannot..."

"Be."

"It is," Andie said. "My name is Andie Rogers, princess of the dragonborn. I wouldn't have come here if this weren't something critical to the survival of my people."

"Please..."

"Follow..."

"Us..."

"Most..."

"Revered..."

"Princess."

The priests turned and began to walk back by the way they came. Andie followed without hesitation, hoping the sooner she found out what they knew the sooner she can leave this place. Oren and the four dragonborn warriors that accompanied them followed. The priests led them deep into the Church, through more hidden doors that spilled open and rooms massive and brilliant. So far, they'd seen no other people besides the priests, but soon they came to a room that must have been at least a kilometer wide. The room was filled with wonderful, warm smells and Andie realized that the entire room was a kitchen and the thousands of people there were all cooking. Her eyes wandered over the dishes and she saw foods she could neither describe nor comprehend.

"What is that?" Andie asked, pointing to a peculiar looking dish.

"Our..."

"Specialty."

"A..."

"Serving..."

"Of..."

"Cloud."

Andie took a closer look and, sure enough, the dish was translucent and waving sedately. Yet it wasn't just a piece of cloud. They'd done something to it. Andie shuddered and turned. She noticed the cooks' faces were covered with the same red sand as the priests'.

"How do they see?" she asked.

"Our..."

"God..."

"Shows..."

"Us..."

"The..."

"Way."

Andie looked at Oren, who already had his hand on his sword. The priests hadn't done or said anything untoward, yet Andie felt something off about them. Something sinister. Andie had learned to trust her instincts and just then they were telling her to prepare for an unpleasant surprise.

The priests led them out of the kitchen and into a room considerably smaller than the others. The priests abruptly stopped and turned toward Andie, who nearly drew her sword she was so startled. She took a quick glance around the room, but there was nothing to see. It was completely empty. For a moment, the priests just stood there, their translucent robes billowing around them, which was odd because there was no wind.

"What..."

"Did..."

"You..."

"Expect..."

"To..."

"Find?"

"Nothing," Andie said, stepping back in response to their tone. "We told you all we want is information. We know nothing about you and your Church."

"That..."

"Much..."

"Is..."

"Clear…"

"Little…"

"Princess."

Andie realized that something was different about the room, something beautiful. It was the hymn. Her spell wasn't working there. She could hear the hymn and it was louder, more persuasive. It was hypnotizing.

"If there's something you want to say then speak up," she said, finding her courage. "We're not here to fight, but it seems you want to provoke us. I suggest you start talking or show us the way out, but if you continue like this I can guarantee you won't like how it ends."

"Finally."

"The…"

"Future…"

"Queen…"

"We…"

"Seek."

Andie was about to ask them what that meant when the men began to levitate. As if that wasn't troubling enough, the men began to merge. All six into one body. And still the hymn flowed into her ears. As she looked at her fellow dragonborn, she could tell the song was getting to them, too.

CHAPTER THREE

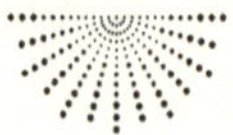

"At the Church of Stone and Sea we seek one thing and one thing only: the unity of all people." The new entity spoke with the voices of all six, its voice hollow and layered and echoed throughout the surrounding space. "All people believing as we do. All people united under our banner. All people wearing the red sand. We felt your power from afar, Andie Rogers. The very walls here desire you. Only you can realize the dream that we have dreamt for centuries. Too long have we subsisted on merely taking the chance passersby who get caught in our hymn. We want the world, which you can deliver. You ask if we know of your enemies and the answer is yes. We have been in contact with all groups that wish you ill. No one passes through our region without our knowledge. We have made promises to each, but we wish to deny them. We wish you to be our ally and spread the seeds of the Church across the lands. Imagine: one people, one mind, one goal, one Church."

The hymn pulsed in her ears. It brought her to her knees. It was so beautiful, powerful, and true. Yes, it was true, it must be. Nothing that poetic and melodic could be false. Andie began to see, to understand her place in the coming days and movements of the church. Everything could be so much better, so perfect, if she would only bow to their will.

"What will you say to our proposition princess? Listen to the hymn, the dream. Believe in us and our loving purpose. We only want to bring all people together under a better truth. The broken, crumbling world from which you come does not need to be the world in which you die. Join us. We will take you into our arms and provide the home you desperately seek. We love you already. Be our vessel. Help us, Andie. Save us."

Andie rested on her knees, happy, crying, finding peace within the red sand walls. But the priests' last words sounded similar, reminding her of something. Something she had heard before. Voices calling out to her from some place. Voices in need, crying for her to help them. Save them. The dragonborn. Her people.

The hymn was so beautiful, so strong, but it was

false. It was merely a subliminal ruse meant to attract her to their terrible cause. She began to wake.

"Impossible," the entity said. "No one resists the magnitude of the hymn in this room! Kneel! Join these ranks and become us!"

"Clearly, you've never messed with a dragonborn before."

Andie regained her feet and cast her spell again, only this time she made it infinitely stronger. The hymn left her and her clarity returned. She faced the entity, but before she could raise her hand, he drifted backwards and disappeared into the walls. Andie was about to help the other dragonborn to their feet when the whole room began to tremble. Within seconds, the room began to morph. Andie and the other dragonborn were borne in the air on the red sand. A face appeared in the wall in front of her.

"If you will not join us, you will fall," it said. "We anticipated you would become one of us, but we made other arrangements as well. An army of thousands lies within these walls. The Church of Sand and Stone has offered asylum to all your enemies and they have gathered here to prepare for a battle that will shake the very foundations of your peace. This army grows daily and soon it will be too large for even the dragonborn to defeat. Feast your eyes upon your end."

A large opening appeared in the wall and as she looked through, Andie could see into a room full of soldiers. There were different factions and different races. Andie knew that her worst fear had come true. All their enemies across Noelle had joined together to form one massive army. The opening closed, protecting the soldiers from the spell Andie just cast.

"You've chosen wrong, princess," the entity said.

"No. You have."

Andie raised her palms and emitted wind and light so powerful, the face in the wall blasted away and the room was pushed out from her. She and the dragonborn fell back to the ground, but the others were still under the influence of the hymn. She had to find a way to get them out.

Suddenly, something hit her face so hard that she was thrown across the room. Just when she was about to catch her breath, something hit her again, and then again while she was in midair. She landed on her back and had just enough time to draw her sword and protect herself from the next strike. It was the red sand, acting as if it had a mind of its own. The very walls of the Church were striking out at her. She fought it off with her sword as best she could, but it was nearly impossible to defend herself on her back. She felt the sand of the floor come up around her throat. Then her arms and legs were trapped and sunk into the sand. In the ceiling above, a large point formed in the sand, extremely sharp, and began to descend toward her.

But she wasn't afraid. She and Saeryn had been studying the grimoires for months. Andie learned a few tricks. She exhaled and clenched her body. Instantly she became fire, her entire body turning into a humanoid flame. The sand all around her superheated, turning to glass. She broke it easily and regained her feet. Before the room could launch another attack, Andie raised her arms and sent a pulse of flames out in every direction. The entire room was turned to glass, stuck in its final movement. Andie cast a spell to make the dragonborn float beside her and she levitated herself up with all the force she could muster, sending her heat out above her first.

Several moments later, they burst from the top of the Church into the warm sunlight. The minute the light touched them, the dragonborn regained consciousness. Andie put them down on the roof of the Church and it was only seconds before their dragons came. They all mounted up and took off as fast as they could, thankful to finally be rid of that place.

CHAPTER FOUR

"You don't understand," Andie said. "The army is massive. It already numbers in the thousands and is still growing."

"Oren," Lymir said, still confused. "What did you see?"

"I'm afraid the allure of the hymn was too much for me and my comrades," Oren replied. "It completely overpowered us. If Andie had not been there, my friends and I would be at the mercy of the Church. Andie is the only one who was enough in control of herself to see what was hidden in those walls, though I can assure you the Church is no friend of ours."

"There were always rumors of their megalomania, but never proof," Saeryn said. "We always assumed the rumors were false and that the Church had no enemies, though now it's obvious that it never allowed its detractors to leave. But I don't understand why they think this army will help them achieve their goals."

"It's likely both the army and the Church are using each other." Andie rubbed her temples as she processed the memory of what she had experienced in the Church. "The Church thinks the army will help it convert the world. The army probably thinks the Church's only goal is to help them take us out. But they're both our enemies. Not only is that army composed of all our enemies, but it's so much closer than we ever imagined. I doubt they have transportation for an army that large, so they'll be walking. It's only a few days by dragon, which means maybe a month on foot with a large army. And I have to be honest they looked like they're starting soon."

Everyone was quiet. Andie, Saeryn, Lymir, Oren, and several of the high members of the University were in the meeting hall of Lymir's department. Andie and Oren had only been back for an hour, but they wasted no time in warning the others.

"We only just opened the University," Lymir said. "But maybe we should consider closing its doors again. I'd rather postpone and save lives than risk people getting hurt just to prove we aren't afraid."

"We cannot close those doors again." Saeryn's spoke with a finality in her voice. "This university is not just for education. It is a symbol to Arvall and to the world of a new era. It means a great deal to my people as well."

"Saeryn's right," said Andie. "We can't close the doors. We can't give in. Even if we did, it wouldn't change anything. That army isn't for show and it's coming no matter what we do. Closing the school only takes away the hope we just gave everyone."

Lymir leaned back in his chair and locked his fingers. Andie couldn't stop thinking about the Church. She realized that their enemies were greater than they ever thought before. Lymir began to nod his head and everyone knew what he would say.

"So, we stay open. Classes go on as usual and the celebrations will continue as scheduled. We'll tell the people nothing, but we'll take every precaution possible. I want our professors trained harder than ever. I want our defenses increased and expanded. Not just magic, but computers, too. I want every security measure we can think of and when we run out of ideas we're going to call in other people to think up some more. If we're going to keep these doors open, we're going to do everything in our power to protect these people and give them a chance."

"We must," said Oren. "These people have welcomed us into their lives and their city. They've risked a great deal to help us and they've made a new world feel like a home. We cannot lead them into slaughter."

"We won't."

The voice belonged to Raesh. Andie didn't see him come in. In fact, she hadn't seen much of him at all over the previous few months. But as he entered the room and neared the table, Andie focused her eyes elsewhere.

"I promise you, Oren, no one is going to be forgotten or abandoned. I agree we have to open the school and keep this army a secret, but don't worry. We've learned a lot in fighting the University. We're ready, and if we're not then we will be."

A kind of ease passed through the room. Raesh had a way of reassuring people. The meeting ended. Andie was almost gone when Raesh called to her.

"Andie."

"Hi," she said, facing him. "Something wrong?"

"I want to talk to you."

Raesh left the room through the other door and Andie followed, wondering what she was supposed to say to him. They hadn't had a real conversation in over six months and whenever they did talk it was only a passing greeting. She followed him down the long main hall, past Leabharlann, and she almost broke off and ran several times, but she didn't. She couldn't. Truth be told, she wanted to talk to him more than anything. So much was going so wrong so fast that she needed someone to confide in.

Saeryn had been a terrific friend, but Raesh got Andie in ways she didn't even get herself. More than that, there had always been something in their way— an enemy, or battle, or catastrophe, or death. Maybe now they could begin to change that. Soon they exited the University through the front doors and walked to the cliff facing the city.

"I don't know if you've been avoiding me or if I've been avoiding you," he began. "What I do know is that sooner or later we're going to have to talk. I want it to be now."

"Raesh, I don't know what you expect me to say," Andie said, berating herself for being so cold. "Whatever this is or was, whatever we are, there just isn't time for it right now. We have enemies all across Noelle. Some of them pretty close to our front door. That's what we need to focus on."

"Is it?"

"Yes. We need to look for ways to root these threats out."

"Do we?"

"Yes."

Raesh simply stood there, watching her in that way of his, that way that no one else on the face of the planet watched her. Andie didn't want to admit it, but she felt a host of emotions she hadn't been forced to deal with in months. After the attack on the city, there was so much chaos and death that she had easily put her personal feelings aside. But now, even with the army in the north, the dragonborn and the citizens of Arvall have gotten control of their lives. There weren't enough distractions.

"There aren't enough distractions to keep you occupied," Raesh said. "And there's nothing out here but us. I'm going to make this as simple as I can for you."

Raesh took two steps toward her, closed her in his arms, and kissed her.

"You're stronger, my leader," said Lucas. "Soon you'll be stronger than you ever were, even before the fight. Now that pieces of the armor have fused with your body, you're going to be more than you ever dreamed. Nearly unstoppable."

"What are we doing here?" Ashur asked, continuing his pushups. "This is a complete and total waste of time. If I'd known this is what you had in mind—"

"Be patient with me, my leader. I'd already sent scouts ahead to speak with these people and the way seems clear. I would've come myself, but I didn't trust your care to anyone else. I've done my research on these people."

"Lucas, tons of people hate the dragonborn, but that doesn't mean we can trust them."

"My leader, you're right. Many people and factions across Noelle are no friends of the dragonborn, but most of them have only ever hated them on principle. Because that was the way they were raised and told to feel. Few people truly hate the dragonborn and their dragons, and my gut tells me that the only people in the world who hate them as much as we do are these people. We're here because we need their numbers and their experience. Chancellor Mharú was smart enough to only show part of his forces that night of the attack. He had battalion members stationed all over Noelle, but even with all of them, we still don't have the force to take on the dragonborn and western Noelle. I believe these people can help us."

Ashur stopped his pushups and stood. He paced, then he turned to face Lucas. Lucas was his second, his most trusted. While Ashur was too injured to command, Lucas intuited his every need and coordinated the battalion in his stead. He aided Ashur in his recovery and never, not even once, gave Ashur any reason to distrust him. Ashur placed a hand on each of his shoulders.

"Forgive me, Lucas. You've been a true ally to me

and I've repaid you with mistrust. I'll meet with them."

Ashur and Lucas walked out into the sun. The top captains of the battalion lived in the largest of a series of cabins the battalion built when it was settled. Just that morning they relocated there, to the Unnamed Lands in east central Noelle, too far for the dragonborn to hear rumors. The sun was going down behind them, and, in front of them, at a distance of two kilometers is the Hushed Forest, so named for the quick and silent death that usually meets those who enter. The trees there were huge, as tall as fifty meters, and more beautiful and lush than any other forest in Noelle. So many have died by thinking that nothing so enchanting could be deadly.

"Are you sure this is where they are?" Ashur asked. "And if they're so deadly, then why did they send our scouts back alive?"

"Three scouts came back."

"How many did you send?"

"Six."

"Maybe we're on to something."

"My leader," said one of the captains. "The information you requested about the Hot Salts has come back."

"The Hot Salts?" Lucas asked. "What could we possibly need there?"

"I started this investigation long before we

confronted the dragonborn that night in Arvall. The Hot Salts is a very inhospitable land: hardly anything grows, most of the water is undrinkable, even the wildlife escaped there in the last age. The only thing that lives in the Hot Salts are criminals, vagrants, and some other undesirable specimens of Noelle. I began to get reports saying they were fleeing the land by the droves, leaving all their possessions. I wondered. What's terrifying enough to displace an entire community of criminals? I started studying topographical maps. There are mountains in the Hot Salts, some of the only mountains around that are high enough and large enough to hide an entire race of people who don't want to be found."

"But the weather there is too unforgiving. The lighting strikes make permanent habitation nearly impossible. Even the criminals only lived at the borders."

"That almost deterred me, but then I realized that those mountains are huge. So huge, in fact, that their summits breach the clouds. If someone were to settle in the mountains above the clouds, no one would ever even think to look for them up there. I've been trying to figure out where the dragonborn have settled since they came out of that portal. They've been careful, but I think I've found them."

"That's excellent news, my leader. These people will be glad to hear it."

"I'm sure they will. What did you say they call themselves?"

"CAN YOU SEE THEM, OLTHRION?"

"Yes, my liege. They can be no further than two kilometers. Do you take them at their word?"

"I trust no one. This so-called battalion claims to hate the dragonborn. They say they wish to see the end of them. I think they also intend to use us."

"What a pity for them, my liege."

"What a pity indeed. No one uses the Beautiful Dead."

CHAPTER FIVE

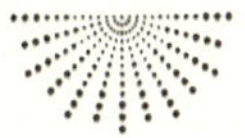

ANDIE STOOD IN VICTORY GARDEN ON THE SIDE OF Brie, waiting for her first class to arrive. She wasn't as nervous as she thought she'd be. At least not about teaching. She and a few other dragonborn worked to reorganize the gardens and introduce some of the plants the dragonborn brought from the past and from the Hot Salts. She was a little worried about the Church, the army, and the battalion, but today those threats seemed far away. Today she was thinking about what happened yesterday and what it felt like to finally be with Raesh. She'd essentially given up hope. She'd even stop trusting that they belonged together. But that was over now. And for the first time in a long time, she was happy.

Soon enough her students arrived and surrounded her. It was time for her very first class to begin.

"Good morning, class. I'm Andie Rogers. Welcome to Modern Horological Enchantment."

Her students stared at her as if she were a celebrity. That was something she hadn't anticipated.

"Excuse me, Ms. Rogers," a girl asked. "Is it true you took down both the Chancellor and the leader of the battalion single-handedly?"

"No. Well, yes, but I learned a tremendous amount from the dragonborn and I had a whole network of people who helped me along the way. Taking down the University was more than just one fight."

"But you're, like, unstoppable."

Several of the students nodded and looked as if they might burst from excitement. Andie felt proud, but also a little overwhelmed.

"No one is unstoppable," she said. "But you can fortify your mind and your abilities by knowing about the options available to you, which is one of the things we'll do in this class. Plant magic might seem lame or uninteresting, maybe not even worth learning, but consider this: when the Chancellor wanted to kill those eight hundred diplomats at the Winter Festival last year he did it by using a crossbred plant species. I know because I helped breed them."

The students finally settled down and their faces become completely sober. Andie didn't want to scare them, but to impress upon them the gravity of what they could learn there and of the world they lived in.

"Ms. Rogers," another student began. "Are we learning how to fight so that we can take on the enemies threatening Arvall?"

Andie looked at the boy, who couldn't be more than sixteen and who was so fragile-looking she feared a strong wind could blow him over. He looked anxious, unsure. They all did. Andie realized that by taking away their excitement, their joy to be learning from her, she'd exposed their fear. It was the same fear the whole city was trying to mask. But she knew she couldn't tell them the truth. They'd decided in the meeting that they would keep everything secret. She must lie.

"Don't worry. No one's coming to the city. You're perfectly safe."

She turned their attention back to horological magic and introduced them to the topics and books they would be studying. She gave them a tour of Victory. She found herself ashamed to be so good at misleading them, at giving them hope that will more than likely prove false. Yet it also felt good to see them smile and hear them laughing and looking forward. The class soon ended and Andie took a moment to celebrate her first teaching experience. Then the next class came. She had to begin lying all over again.

Soon the day was done. Andie grabbed a few things from her office and boarded SKY 6 to the city. Once the train reached the bottom, she boarded another train to cross the city, then another to Michaelson. Once there, she paid a visit to her old home. She didn't have the heart to sell it or have it taken down. Instead, she paid to have it cleaned regularly, though she knew she would probably never live there again. The house was all she had left of her parents, though. Her mother who was murdered for being different and her father who died because Andie was too angry to take care of him properly. She shed a few tears and then boarded the Sud to Taline.

By the time she reached the city, night had fallen. She caught a cab in front of the station. Her cell rang.

"Hi," Raesh's voice echoed through the receiver. "I didn't see you leave today."

"I'm sorry. I just wanted to get over to Taline before it got late. I wanted to make visiting hours."

"It's okay. I was just there a couple days ago."

"It's not fair."

There was a moment of silence while the weight of the situation hung.

"I love that you're still going," Raesh said. "I know it's hard and I know how much you want a miracle. I want one, too."

"Let's talk about something else. How was your first day?"

"Great," he said. "I think the students really responded to the lesson. I wasn't sure about giving them an assignment on the first day, but they seemed really into the idea of research. I can't believe I taught four classes today. You?"

"Well, us mere nomags can only handle two classes a day, but it was pretty amazing. I never thought I could warm to teaching so easily. I feel honored to be responsible for someone else's knowledge."

"I'm sure you're going to have a great year. You're kind of like royalty there. Everyone wants to know you. Professors, students. I heard some janitors mooning over you..."

"Ha. Ha. I didn't ask to be famous."

"True, but you do it well. I snuck in your class to see you this afternoon."

"What did you think?"

"I thought you were amazing and that you looked more beautiful than anyone or anything I've ever seen."

"As far as compliments go, that's definitely a top contender."

"I mean it. I'm so happy you stopped hiding the color of your hair and eyes. And not just that, but your energy. Your drive. Everything about you. You're perfect, Andie."

"If I say it back now it's just going to sound stupid," she said.

"Don't worry about it. I already know I'm perfect."

She laughed as the cab pulled up at The Letter, the largest hospital in western Noelle. When Andie was a child it was destroyed in a terrorist attack, but had since been rebuilt and made bigger and stronger than ever. It was rebuilt out of the most advanced loveglass, and was virtually impossible to infiltrate or attack. Andie felt a weight coming over her heart as she looked up at the massive structure.

"Okay," she said. "I'm here."

"Alright. Call me when you're done."

"Okay. I'll probably just stay at a hotel tonight. It's too late to take a train back and I probably won't feel like making the trip anyway."

"No problem. I'll just see you tomorrow afternoon. Talk to you soon."

Andie hung up and exited the car. It was a slow walk because she was thinking of all the things that place represented. She had to go through a few security checkpoints, but it was really a quick process, especially since everyone in western Noelle knew who she was. She caught the elevator to the seventy-seventh floor and walked to the end of the hall. When she entered the room, it was as if the breath had left her body. It happened to her every time.

Carmen lay in bed, unresponsive, as she had been since the explosion in the Hot Salts. The doctors said her coma was unlike anything they'd ever seen. They'd tried so many treatments and methods that Andie had lost count. The problem was due in large part to the fact that no one was quite sure what spells the Chancellor was sending through Marvo's body. The spellwork was foreign to them, and, with both the Chancellor and Marvo dead, there was no way to test. Carmen had been lying in that bed in Taline for months. The doctors said that if she didn't wake up on her own, she'd never wake up at all.

Andie walked around the bed to the side facing the window. She sat down on the bed next to her friend and put another chocolate bar in the top drawer of the bedside table. She brought Carmen's favorite candy every time she came to visit. All three drawers were almost full. She saw the new flowers that Raesh brought the last time he was there. Overwhelmed by thought of how much Raesh himself must be handling the loss of his family, her stomach clenched in tight knots.

Andie took Carmen's hand and kissed her cheek, trying to remember what the old days were like before the University ruined everything.

"Oh, Ms. Rogers, it's you." The calm voice of a nurse spoke through the doorway as she carried in a small tray of medical supplies.

"Hi, Alecia. Long day?"

"They're all long. You? You look pretty chipper tonight."

"First day teaching and it went surprisingly well. Has she had many visitors today?"

"Not today. Most days she usually does. Dragonborn, council fighters, old friends from Arvall. Actually, there was someone here earlier. They didn't stay long. Kind of creeped me out to be honest."

"Why? Did they do anything?"

"Not particularly. They were just... odd. They were dressed in all black and stood in the far corner without saying a word. They didn't stay long and didn't say anything, but they seemed, I don't know, dangerous. More like they were spying on her than checking on her."

"I'll keep an eye out. Send word to me if you see them again."

"I sure will, sweetheart. You have a good night. And don't worry about visiting hours, stay as long as you like."

Alecia left and Andie bagan to wonder about who could be spying on Carmen and why. It was one more thing she never thought of. Carmen was a huge part of the resistance, and she fought fiercely alongside Andie and the others. If anyone wanted revenge, they could simply come to The Letter and kill Carmen while she lay there defenseless. Or worse yet, they could take her and hold her for ransom, allowing them to get almost anything from Andie and her friends. She made a mental note to increase the security on Carmen's hallway.

"Hi, gorgeous," she said, stroking Carmen's hair. "I know, I was just here the other day, but I missed you. I was kind of hoping you'd take pity on me and wake up. I'm sure you've got a whole host of insults and blunt talk you've been storing up while you rest. I don't think I can take it all at once, but if you spread it out evenly over, say, a week, I'm sure I can handle it. What do you say? You up for a reunion?

"I get it. No hard feelings. You're just not ready yet. I mean, honestly, I wouldn't be in a hurry to get back here either, not with all these... never mind. That can wait. I don't know if Raesh told you this, but... we're together. Together together. I know what you're thinking: why did it take so long? I just wanted you to be the first to know it and to know that I'm happier now than I've ever been. I know there's so much going on in the world, so many things to watch out for, but he makes me so ridiculously happy. And I trust him completely. Which is why you need to wake up so you can berate me for still not having told him I love him when I've known it for so long now.

"Where are you now? Somewhere peaceful, I hope. You deserve it. It's hard to imagine where we came from and who we use to be. Almost as hard as it is to imagine where we're headed. I don't think you realize how much we need you. Not just your skill and your power, but your light. Your determination. Your mostly inappropriate jokes. I never realize how much I need you until I'm here. But hey, no pressure. You come back whenever you're ready."

She held Carmen's hand. Minutes passed, then hours. Nurses and doctors came and went, having brief and hushed conversations with Andie and giving her updates on Carmen's condition, if they could even really be called updates. The moon came up in the night sky and Andie tried to watch the stars, but the lights of the city were too bright. Instead of getting a room in the city, Andie stayed in the room with Carmen.

CHAPTER SIX

THE NEXT MORNING, SHE KISSED CARMEN'S CHEEK and said goodbye. She made it back to the University just in time to receive her first class of the day. Tuesdays and Thursdays she taught Plant-Based Poisons to the 3rd and 4th Cycles. The students seemed to like the material and her teaching, and the day went by without a hitch. She had two more classes, and, aside from the students' inability to get past her celebrity, she'd consider her day a success.

After class, she walked to the second east wing of the University and waited for Raesh to finish his class. He came out looking pleased.

"Good day?" she asked, kissing his cheek.

"Yeah. Do your students stare at you like you're royalty?"

"Oh, so you have that, too…"

Together they walked to the main hub and caught SKY 1 up through the mountain to the faculty living spaces. The train went much slower than SKY 6, but Andie enjoyed this ride more. Everything on the train was free, and rather than going straight up through the rock of the mountain—which would have risked the structural integrity of the entire summit—SKY 1 went a few hundred feet straight up and then exited to the side of Brie, where it ascended to the top by traveling around and around the summit at a steady incline. They'd caught it at just the right time because the sun was just going down over Arvall. Raesh held Andie's hand as they watch.

"Quite a view," he said.

"If you're into gorgeous sunsets and vivid, sprawling colors."

"I already know the answer, but—"

"No change. She's still in a coma and they still have no idea what to do for her. But she looks good, if that means anything."

"It means enough."

"I can't believe you tricked me into moving in with you," Andie said, grinning.

"Tricked? You and I remember things very differently. But if you truly feel that strongly about it, there's plenty of other spaces available on the mountaintop. Feel free to move along."

"I never said I had an issue with being tricked. Unless you think we're moving too fast?"

"We should've been together the day we met. Let's be honest: the lives we lead aren't the safest. When I think of all the time we've wasted and the people we've lost, the things we've seen and the enemies that are still coming... no, I don't think we're moving too fast. I don't think we're moving fast enough."

He kissed her cheek and Andie didn't say it, but she agreed with him completely. In a world where so much was out of her control, Racsh was at least something that she wanted that she could have. No matter what threats showed themselves in the future, nothing could change the way she and Raesh felt about each other. The train continued its journey around the mountain until it finally reached the summit. Andie and Raesh descended and made their way back into the mountain through the tunnel.

The professors' living spaces were, in a word, sumptuous. No expense had been spared in the construction, decoration, or furnishing. They had the best of everything, despite Andie's instruction to allocate resources elsewhere during construction. The University may have been completely heinous, but they took care of their instructors, and now all of that luxury belonged to the new professors. Any dragonborn-hating propaganda had been ejected, but there was still enough luxury to go around. Everything was made from gold, silver, and even jewels. The rugs and paintings and fixtures had been brought from the farthest and most decadent corners of Noelle. Even the floors were made of platinum loveglass, a material so expensive and so rare that most people never came within a hundred kilometers of it in their lives. The opulence truly couldn't be overstated.

"I still can't believe we live here," Raesh said. "I know we got rid of all the propaganda and anything that even remotely resembled sympathy or acceptance of the University's actions, but, I don't know, sometimes I just feel like…"

"Like we should burn the whole place down and dump the ashes in the Spider Sea? Yeah. That idea was discussed. In depth. But ultimately this is just stuff. Really, really nice stuff that has nothing to do with hatred or evil. Actually, we checked the records and most of this stuff was actually sent as gifts. Regardless, I see no reason to be mad at diamonds. They didn't do anything to me."

"Fair."

"Now let's talk about the meeting with Lymir and Oren."

"Oren's getting ready to fly back to the Hot Salts and get the dragonborn army ready. He's concerned the location of the dragonborn might not be secure. To be honest, I agree with him. I think it's safest to assume that nothing is safe anymore."

"Tell me about it. Alecia was telling me last night that some stranger was spying on Carmen. Don't worry, I had them increase the security detail and keep a closer eye on the camera, but I'm beginning to realize that we have too many people who are important to us spread over too great a distance."

"Agreed. Oren and Saeryn decided it might be best to move all the dragonborn to Brie until further notice. It should work out fine, since half of the dragonborn are already here or in Arvall anyway. They would've consulted you, but—"

"They knew I'd agree anyway."

"Right. Lymir's working on a new training program for the professors. He'd like to train a few students, too. Anyone who shows promise and proves themselves to be discreet. We've reached out to some militia in western Noelle, but we haven't heard back yet. Taline has promised us whatever we need, including soldiers. I think we've got as much of a handle on this thing as possible right now. Have you been in contact with Marcus Iceubes?"

"Yeah, I spoke with him between classes today. He's still pouring over the journals I found. I was worried there might not be as much in them as I thought, but, apparently, he can't research fast enough.

He's pulling out hundreds of secrets every week. I know there's got to be something in there that can help us in this war. He's going to give his classes over to a colleague so he can spend more time with the pages. He seems hopeful. And Saeryn and I are still studying grimoires, at least those we can read. We need a translator, but it has to be someone we trust. I know we hoped things might be worked out diplomatically, but I think it's safe to say that's never going to happen."

"We never have time to celebrate one victory before it's right back to battle."

"Yeah. Life sucks like that."

In their apartment, they dropped their things by the door and made their way to the couch. Raesh laid down and then Andie fell in his arms, her face against his chest.

"Well," she said. "Let's get ready to win a war."

THE DAYS PASSED SLOWLY. Andie, Raesh, Lymir, and the other professors began training at night on the summit. Many of them were smart, driven, and fully aware of the danger they faced, but few of them had ever been in a fight. Raesh called all the fighters that once fought alongside his father to help train the professors and select students.

Before the fighters returned to Arvall, they had been on assignment in and around the String Fields. Their mission was to gather intelligence on any threats in the region, but the Beautiful Dead and anyone else who'd been hiding near the border had evaded capture. The fighters had not learned much other than that the Beautiful Dead had taken every man, woman, and child from several small towns nearby and taken their resources. News of the deed spread quickly, and the city, the entire region, began to get suspicious. The fighters did succeed in wiping out several small factions on their way to join the army in the Church of Stone and Sea. They'd brought back one from each faction and the professors had learned a great deal about the army's capabilities and attack methods. Andie had been right. The army was already on its way and would reach Arvall in less than a month. The fighters also caught the trail of the battalion, but it was deemed too risky to follow. No one really knew what the battalion was up to or what it was capable of.

Lymir and Saeryn worked tirelessly to keep peace and hope in the city. Thankfully, the people still trusted the University and the dragonborn. Lymir instituted programs to make the citizens of the city aware without forcing them into fear. Saeryn sent word to her people to prepare themselves and not to take the secrecy of their location for granted. Saeryn spent her days as a liaison between the humans and sorcerers of Arvall and the dragonborn, though relations had never been better. She spent her nights pouring over the grimoires and the histories, trying to learn what useful spells she could and to decipher where the Beautiful Dead were. As a Queen, her integrity and strength were unparalleled, especially since she now bore the burden of not just her people, but the city of Arvall as well.

Oren remained among the dragonborn in the Hot Salts of Mithraldia. Not a day went by that he didn't worry about his Queen and princess so far away, and about all the dragonborn and the terrible fight they face with the Dead. More than that, his experience in the Church of Stone and Sea haunted him. It was a very rare thing for a dragonborn to be overcome by tricks, enchanted stone or not. He questioned his ability to command his dragon, to protect his people. He knew that Andie could not always be around to watch out for him. Or for anyone else. He spent a great deal of time preparing the dragonborn for their exodus and fortifying the mountaintop, so that even though they must eventually leave, they would still have a home to come back to.

In Taline, Stefan prepared himself and his city for the attack he knew would come. They had only just been able to breathe again, finally rid of the University's theft and terrorism. Now they found themselves plunged right back into life and death circumstances. But Stefan was no fool, and he had been around long enough to know how to defend himself with the utmost fury. He left no stone unturned in his search for the threats to his city, and he made sure of every bit of his considerable knowledge to make the city as safe as possible. As a personal favor to Andie, he had increased security measures on the seventy-seventh floor of The Letter and he went over himself every afternoon to ensure that Carmen was protected.

Raesh practiced controlling his magic. While he did improve some, there was only so much control a pearlblood could hope for. His biggest accomplishment was finding other pearlbloods in western Noelle. There weren't many—in fact, there were likely less than a hundred in the entire world—but they were strong. They appeared to have been practicing their magic in secret. Raesh found comfort in being surrounded by similar people, but he never stopped thinking of his father and how much he had to live up to. He knew there was nothing he could have done, but in saving other lives he could make his father proud.

Classes continued as usual and the professors were careful to keep the secret. The students seemed to truly love everything they were learning and—besides the usual lethargy, tardiness, and excuses that plagued every campus—the new and improved university was running better than ever. Andie and Raesh's classes were going well and Lymir's leadership steered the institution in a new and promising direction. If it weren't for the threat of impending doom, life might just have been perfect.

CHAPTER SEVEN

"You've made us wait for days," Ashur said. "I understand you don't know us or our agenda, but I would think the least you could do is show us some common courtesy. We're here to offer you the help you so desperately need."

"Forgive me, Ashur, but—"

"Where I come from, Olthrion, the lesser address the superior by their proper rank. Call me commander."

"And where I come from, such disrespect can lead one rather quickly to an early deposition. As I was saying, we made you wait not out of pettiness, but security. It would be foolish to pretend that we were afraid of you, but we do nothing without knowing who we're dealing with and what they're capable of. We know who you are. What are you capable of?"

As he turned from Olthrion, Ashur grinned. He motioned for his battalion to stand aside. He tensed his body and felt the power of his magic being amplified and focused by his new armor. He raised his hand and then slammed it into the ground. The moment his palm collided with the soil, an explosion flowed through his hand and split the ground for fifty yards. It was so wide and deep that several of the gargantuan trees lost their balance and topple over inside.

"That's just a taste of what I can do. My entire battalion is powerful and highly trained in combat. And more than anything else, we hate the dragonborn."

"Do you?"

It wasn't Olthrion who spoke, but another, deeper voice. Half of the battalion took a step back just at the sound of it. The man made his way to the front of the group and stood directly across from Ashur. He was tall, wrapped in impressive muscle, and his hair and beard were long and sleek. He carried no weapon, and yet he seemed more dangerous than any other person Ashur had met.

"You must be the King," Ashur said.

"There are no Kings here, commander. We follow the strongest and I have been the strongest for a very long time. My people have followed my lead for nearly a century."

"That's impossible," Ashur said, taking a closer look at him. "You can't be more than thirty years old. Men don't live that long."

"But I am not a man. Even if I look like one. My race is very old and very powerful. We've made it our mission to be invisible and there are precious few people living who know what we are and what we want. I'm curious as to how you know of us."

"Chancellor Myamar Mharú. Before he died he told me that his family had been keeping up with your people since the beginning of the first age. The secret was passed down through generations in case you were ever needed. He would have come himself, but he was murdered by the dragonborn. I know what you want and how you can obtain it. An army grows in the north that will march on the city of Arvall. We won't be able to make it back in time for the battle, but that's not what matters. By the time we get there the army will most likely have failed, but the dragonborn and the city will be weak. And from there we'll crush them."

"I cannot claim to dislike the strategy. Letting the eager fools go in first to weaken the foundation and die in the process, and then you and your battalion come in to knock down the house the dragons have built. Admirable. But I think you underestimate the men marching from the Church."

"Do you honestly think a group of poor, half-trained guerilla fighters can really band together and take out Arvall and the dragons? They have the numbers, but I've fought the dragonborn. It'll take more than numbers. It'll take fierce training and unimaginable power."

"Which is why I sent a dozen of my greatest warriors there months ago. By the time that army leaves the Church they will be worthy of a battle with those blood traitors. Make no mistake, commander, my people and I have hoped for the day when the dragonborn would return and be within our reach again. We've left nothing to chance, not even you. You think it was your idea to come here? I had spies slip information about my people into your Chancellor's office. All we had to do was wait for his greed and corruption to engulf him. He sought us out long before his death. I promised him an end to the dragonborn in exchange for his battalion and his resources. You didn't seek me out, young Ashur. You're here because you were promised to me, because you're part of a much larger and older game than you realize. Did you really think that fool Mharú would have been capable of all the things he accomplished if I hadn't given him the ideas? Who do you think convinced that elitist, xenophobic Church to harbor the army in the first place?"

"You're saying you've had a hand in everything that's happened?"

"Nothing has happened since the dragonborn stepped out of that portal that I haven't known about. We were the ones who told the factions to join as one."

"Then I'm in the right place. But I know something you don't."

"And what's that?"

"I know where the dragonborn home is."

A guttural breath traveled through the man, Olthrion, and all their people. The battalion members looked up and around them, finally noticing they were surrounded. The people were not just in front of them, they were in the trees, peering down with fierce frowns and keen eyes. They were impressively built, agile, strong, men and women alike. More than that, the people were surprisingly beautiful. In fact, it was hard to look away from them. They were wild and fierce and terrifying, but also breathtakingly perfect. Even the silver-haired elders had no problem hanging among the branches.

"Now you have my attention, commander," the man said.

"Your people go by many names and countless legends follow you. I know now I wouldn't have found you unless you wanted me to. This isn't even where you live, is it? Just another smokescreen."

"Bravo."

"The truth is that no one really knows anything

about you anymore. You're nothing more than a myth. I'll gladly give you the location of the dragonborn and then follow you into this great war, but I need to know you can deliver your end of the deal. I know you're intelligent, cunning, intimidating, and apparently great at aging well, but what can you do for us?"

The man didn't look offended, but rather like he was glad to have been asked to exhibit his skill. His fellows cleared the space around him and he smiled.

"We are an ancient race, filled with the might of gods and beasts."

He ran to a tree almost too quick for Ashur to see and smashed his fist in a swiping strike, cutting the tree in half with absolute ease.

"We are the terrors between night and day that frighten time itself and break the hands of fate."

He leapt into the air and kicked his feet against the tree trunk, knocking the tree backward and flipping through the air, catching himself on another tree by punching his hand through the bark.

"We are strong, agile, fast, our senses keener than all the fiercest natural predators combined. We can hear conversations a whole town away, see through two kilometers of darkness, smell blood across mountains, feel the weather change even before the clouds change. Nothing we hunt escapes."

He released the tree and landed with a force that shook the ground.

"We live for centuries. We are the true children of the dragon. The beasts that bred us can no more hurt us than they can the blood traitors. If a dragon were to breathe fire on me this very moment, I would not even feel the flames. We are the greatest threat to the world. The true question is not whether we can deliver, but whether you can keep up."

"Impressive," Ashur said.

"We find you impressive as well, commander. We would not have invited you here if we didn't. I kept a close eye on your training and the battle in Arvall. Your strategy, intelligence, and leadership are impressive. Your combat and magic are remarkable."

"Speaking of magic, where's yours?"

"Don't worry. We shall have it soon enough."

"I think we're on the same page. With my battalion and your abilities, I think the dragonborn, the traitors, are as good as dead. Only one thing is left. What do I call you?"

"My name... is Beladorion."

<hr>

"WE NEED MEDICAL ATTENTION. NOW!"

Andie heard the yelling from Victory. She told her students to stay put and rushed to the hallway to see what had happened.

"We couldn't take him to any hospital in the city. We were afraid of spreading panic."

Andie finally made it to the commotion and saw who was talking. It was Sarinda. Andie hadn't seen her since the day of the explosion in the Hot Salts. Raesh told her that Sarinda had been on assignment in the Dark Tundra, and, since she left there, no one had heard from her. Andie felt like hugging her, but Sarinda was one of four people carrying a bloodied body and there were more bodies following. They headed down the hall and through the main hub until they reached the medical wing. The doctors came out and took the bodies in. Sarinda turned to Andie and gave a little sight of relief. They threw their arms around each other.

"Come with me," Andie said.

She led Sarinda back outside and over to a secluded area where they could have some privacy. Sarinda was still breathing irregularly and sweating, but she looked as if she'd be fine.

"Are you hurt? Do you need a doctor?" Andie asked.

"No, just a few scrapes and bruises. I was lucky. We never saw them coming, Andie."

"Saw who?"

"I still don't know. It was a small phalanx, roughly a hundred soldiers, probably a scouting party. Is there something going on I missed?"

"We're about to be at war, Sarinda. There's a massive army marching down from the north right now. Didn't you see them?"

"No, we only saw those hundred."

"Tell me everything that happened."

"We left the Dark Tundra two months ago. We'd chased the battalion all over the north of Noelle, almost across the pole to the Old World, and finally defeated them. Or at least the faction we'd been chasing. We left the cold and came by ship down along the coast, but we were delayed because of icebergs in the Pauper's Sea and attacks from marauders. That's why we've been out of touch for so long because they destroyed our communications. We finally got free and then went full steam ahead to make up the time. Near the Church of Stone and Sea we saw a lot of movement, but we just figured it was another one of their mass rituals. We hit the Spider Sea and decided to dock in King's Harbor. But as soon as we stepped off the ship, we came under attack. They had weapons we'd never seen or heard of before. It was a bloodbath, but we killed three times as many of them. There were only about thirty of us, but we defeated them, barely. We had no idea what was happening."

"Did you get all of them?"

"All except one. Andie, I don't think he was human. He was strong and fast. He moved unlike anyone I've ever seen before. It was like he was driven by pure hate. We almost had him pinned down, but he escaped. He said something odd."

"What?"

"He said he wouldn't die before he'd killed his share of blood traitors. I don't know if he was crazy or if he was playing a part in a larger game than we realized."

"Sarinda, that was no fluke. That was an advanced party for the army that's marching on us. They must've thought you were an advanced party, too. And if that man was who I think he was, he wasn't crazy. He's one of the Beautiful Dead."

"The what?"

"They're the other race descended from dragons and they want to kill every dragonborn and drink our blood so they can obtain our magic. And the Church of Stone and Sea isn't just a neutral spectator anymore. They almost killed me and Oren, and now they're giving all their resources to an army of thousands that's coming to kill every last soul in Arvall City."

"I see I've got a lot to catch up on."

Andie and Sarinda talked for a long time while they waited for news. Sarinda received some attention for her wounds. The half dozen other fighters who survived were being treated somewhere in the hospital, but their condition wasn't critical. Andie sent one of the professors to take over her classes for the day. Eventually, the doctor came to speak to them.

"I'm sorry," he said. "We did as much as we could, but we simply don't have the knowledge to treat this kind of damage. We might have been able to do something if they'd arrived sooner, but by the time they arrived the symbiote had already taken to great a hold, I'm sorry."

"The what?" Sarinda asked.

"The symbiote. It's not fully alive or sentient, but the magic behind it is formidable. The sand has been animated so that it gets in an orifice or laceration and expands as it moves deeper. It absorbed their blood until their hearts stopped."

"The sand?" Andie asked.

"Yes. Red sand. It was hard to tell at first, because of all the blood, but it's definitely red sand."

The doctor turned to leave and Andie and Sarinda immediately ran down the hallway to the operating room. The sight of their fallen comrades lying withered and lifeless made them both halt in place, their bodies unmoving yet their minds racing wildly. Andie could barely comprehend what she was seeing.

While the limbs on the bodies before them were wasted and the skin hanging loose, their midsections were grotesquely swollen where the sand accumulated and soaked up all their blood. Sarinda's tears began to fall as she moved closer to the bodies. These were the people she'd traveled and fought with for months. Andie was close to tears herself as she leaned to inspect the wounds. Some of them looked as if they were cut or stabbed first and the sand got in afterwards, and some looked like they were wounded by the sand itself. But there was no mistaking what has happened.

"I'll kill them all," Andie said.

"What?" Sarinda asked.

"The Church. They've figured out how to weaponize the sand."

CHAPTER EIGHT

LATER IN THE EVENING, AFTER YET ANOTHER MEETING, Andie stood beside Saeryn in silence, thinking of all the ways the world they knew could end. They stood in the Archives, staring down into the portal that brought the dragonborn to the future. This portal has done so much for them and might still do a great deal of trouble.

"I still believe we should destroy this thing," Andie said. "Even the University's founding families were afraid of it. That should tell us all we need to know."

"I fear it, too, Andie. If we are not careful we may be sent back through this doorway just like we came from it. I fear, too, that Sarinda's run-in with the army's advance party will only make them march on us faster."

"Definitely. Now that they know they can not only stand their ground, but kill us, I don't see why they wouldn't want to speed up. They've been planning this for months. We're unprepared. They have an army of thousands and we have a city full of people who've never had to fight."

"I share your worry. Lymir is recruiting more students and now he has all the professors in training, but our numbers are nowhere near where they should be. We certainly have experience and power on our side, but they could overwhelm us with sheer mass."

"It doesn't help that the Dead are with them."

"Actually, I don't think they are, or at least not completely. The Beautiful Dead are cunning and the greatest hunters and warriors the world has ever known. They were already master strategists before our race was even born. It seems...unwise to march with this army. The Dead are certainly bold, but they would never be so guileless as to attack us head on. I don't know how to describe it other than to say they would consider it a bad hunt. No, whatever they're planning you can be sure they won't march with the army, with the exception of a few lesser lieutenants for distraction."

Andie leaned against the wall and looked over at Saeryn.

"I don't understand how you can both be

descended from dragons and not have the same abilities."

"Look at the scales on your arm, princess. They're very light, almost imperceptible, but if you look closely you can make out their shape."

Andie raised her arm and observed her skin as carefully and closely as she could. Before long she saw the pearlescent sheen and the beautiful scales. Upon looking closer, she saw that the scales were not the same shape as the dragons'. They were perfect heptagons.

"They have seven sides."

"Because we were born from the blood of seven dragons. The Dead are descended from only five. And, of course, our progenitors were centuries apart."

"No matter how many times I come face to face with it or how many different shapes it takes I will never understand it."

"What?"

"How much people can hate us."

"Well, we knew something was coming, right?"

"Yes, but not this. Jacobi of House Clio wasn't terribly specific. She wrote that the founding families only used the portal to travel to the future once, to this time, and that they saw a city consumed by war. The journal said that the descendants of dragons destroyed everything."

"Well, at least now we know it was not us they saw, but the Beautiful Dead."

"The journal described the war as the worst and most deadly they'd ever seen. The founding families were monsters who had thousands of men, women, and children killed for no reason at all and even they said this war was horrific. They described it as the end of all things."

"The End of Days," Saeryn said. "Amanna Deireadh. It all makes sense now. The families returned to their own time and told their descendants what they'd seen. Over time the story made the descendants angry and more afraid until hate was all they knew. The mistaken future fueled everything they felt because they thought we were going to end the world. The story itself got twisted and grew into legend so that instead of 'the descendants of dragons' it became 'the dragonborn.'"

"The so-called end of times wasn't the descendants of the dragonborn restoring their race and taking revenge, it was the Dead restoring the power they think we stole from them and taking revenge on us. Are you telling me that the history of Noelle was forged because a few families didn't know how to tell a story?"

"It would appear so."

"Super."

Andie and Saeryn didn't stay in the chamber with

the portal any longer than they had to. It was the only room in the entire university that hadn't been repaired. Everyone thought leaving it to carry the signs of the first battle would be a fitting memorial to everything that followed. She and Saeryn made their way out and moved slowly through Leabharlann, Andie reminiscing on the days when all she had to worry about was searching for a book on the dragonborn. As they exited the massive library, they ran into Marcus in the hallway.

"Professor Iceubes, hello," Saeryn greeted him.

"Your grace," he said. "Andie, I'm glad I've run into you. Both of you, actually."

"Have you found something?" Andie asked.

"Let's take a walk," he said, turning. "The question is what haven't I found. The founding families were keeping secrets from everyone, even each other. You wouldn't believe the people they've had killed, the petty jealousies, the secret wars, the unbelievable amounts of gold and silver they stole from the mint when they took over this building. I can't stop finding things, but I haven't come across anything on the Beautiful Dead. It's almost as if the families didn't even know they existed. But I do have good news. I've found the instructions to operating the portal."

"You mean we can control it now?" Saeryn asked, lighting up in hope.

"I mean we can do whatever we want. Turn it off, turn it on, use it for past, future, teleportation. We can control it, instead of it controlling us."

"That may be the best news we've had all year," Andie said. "Thank you, professor, so much."

"There's more. The families didn't destroy the portals. Collectively they all claimed to have taken responsibility for destroying their appointed lot, but secretly each family kept one and hid it."

"You mean there are six more portals out there?" Saeryn asked, crestfallen.

"Seven," Marcus said. "At least seven. They're all over the place. There's one in New Carthage, one in Thabes in the True Isles. I haven't been able to find them all."

"Great," Andie said. "One step forward, seven steps back."

"I know it's not the news we were hoping for, but it gets worse. I'm not quite through the journals yet, but I doubt there's much more. I know we were hoping for something major, but I think it's essentially a dud."

"But there must be something."

"I'm sorry, Andie, but the truth is the later generations of the families weren't as cunning or ambitious as their ancestors. They didn't seem to have any interest in anything except wealth, prestige, and promiscuity. They certainly don't have any secrets that are going to give us any sort of magical or tactical advantage."

Andie sunk her fingers in her head and closed her eyes. It was not even close to what she was hoping to hear. She felt Saeryn's hand on her shoulder, comforting her. She opened her eyes, so frustrated she was almost crying.

"It's okay, Marcus," she said. "We'll just have to find another way. Thank you for all your help. Just learning how to control the one portal we do have is a help."

"I'll let you know if I find anything else."

Marcus left. Andie turned to Saeryn and put her arms around her. They stayed like that for a moment, comforting each other.

"I was really counting on those journals," Andie said.

"As was I, princess. But there is an aid for us out there somewhere."

"I'm sure you will. I think I'm going to take a walk and clear my head. I'll see you later."

Andie was only walking for a minute before she realized what must be done. It was time. She made her way deliberately, not stopping to talk to anyone or look at anything, just moving forward with her purpose. Everything they'd tried so far had failed. Visiting the Church, hunting the battalion, protecting the city. There were still bombings along the edge of town and messages still appeared in the fields. Every time they poked their heads out, it was only to find they have a new threat. Every line they'd held for hope had dropped them. The journals, the grimoires, their scouting parties. Even the training seemed doomed to fail because the recruits simply weren't tough enough. The enemy army was fast approaching, and, after the skirmish with Sarinda and the fighters, the army was no doubt invigorated, spurred on by the small victory and by the promises of the Church and the Dead.

Andie checked the time on her phone, a slow smile threatening her face. She knew that Lymir's office hours and classes were over, and sped toward his office without a look back.

She found him sitting in his chair, lost in thought.

"Lymir, it's time."

"LADIES AND GENTLEMEN, citizens and dragonborn, thank you for coming," Lymir began. "I want to thank you for your unconditional support and the way you've trusted each other and the University. What I'm going to tell you today is both shocking and unsurprising. It's no secret that people outside of western Noelle aren't happy about the dragonborn return. They haven't had the opportunity to live among the dragonborn and befriend them like we have. They still believe in the old lies and they have no intention of letting go of that hate. My staff and I, as well as the dragonborn warriors, have done our best to keep you sheltered and to protect you from a truth we didn't think you were ready for, a truth that we weren't sure would even come to pass, but it is my sad and heavy to duty to tell you this truth. Factions of heinous people from eastern, northern, and central Noelle have come together to form an army the size of which has not been seen in many cycles. With the help of the Church of Stone and Sea and another very old and powerful enemy, this army intends to make its way to us and destroy us. I ask you to forgive me for keeping this from you. We thought we were doing the best thing to preserve hope, but it is no longer prudent or helpful.

"I don't know if I still have the right to say this to you, but rest assured. The University has already been stocked with weapons, food, and supplies. We started stockpiling necessities before these threats even arose, just as a precaution. I urge you to take refuge in the University and its walls where you will be well protected. If the University reaches capacity, we have shelters and bunkers set up across the city and each and every one of them is well-equipped to withstand a siege. The rest of the dragonborn warriors should be arriving soon and you'll have all the protection you need. I can see you're scared and I won't tell you not to be, but don't for a second think we've abandoned you. Your safety is always paramount. Know, too, that the professors and a large number of students have been receiving specialized training and will be prepared to defend you. I urge you all to do your best to learn what you can in the coming days. We'll need all the help we can get. Work on defending your families, your neighbors. We can survive this.

"I know the future must seem dark and believe me, I am just as afraid as you are. But I'm not going to give in and I'm not going to run. For those of you who wish to get out of the city, do so only if you can do it safely. The enemy is everywhere and they will not hesitate to kill you and everyone you love. I won't lie to you: we face the battle of our lives. But this is far from over. Our great city will not fall. The new university will succeed in its mission. No army of any size will take what is ours. There is always hope."

"IF ANY WARRIOR is left standing mount your dragon and fly for the west! Save whom you can and flee!"

The mountain peak was completely overrun with the Beautiful Dead. They climbed the mountain in the night, unbothered by the lightning and the storms, and breached the clouds just as morning dawned. They were so silent and quick they'd already taken down fifty warriors before the alarm was sounded. They moved with a speed and agility the dragonborn were not ready for. They had forgotten how capable and how terrifying their old enemies could be. Once roused, the dragonborn warriors put up a remarkable defense, but then they were surprised by the appearance of the battalion. Ashur showed no mercy.

Now every warrior left standing raced for their dragon, many being cut down in their stride. Oren was the last line of defense, doing his best to hold off the Dead and the battalion so that his friends could escape to warn the city. Only three dragons managed to take off from the mountain and of those three only one was allowed to escape. The dragonborn could not believe their eyes when the Dead were able to ride their dragons. A single dragonborn warrior became a dot on the horizon as he flew west. Oren continued to fight, cutting down battalion fighters and the Dead alike. He was truly a spectacular warrior, the best and strongest of all the dragonborn army.

But Beladorion appeared. His strength, his speed, his instincts were too much for the already exhausted Oren. With a deft move, he caught Oren on the back of the head and smashed his face into the mountainside. He picked Oren up and landed a series of strikes so fast and fierce and powerful that it was all the bloody dragonborn warrior could do to stay conscious. Beladorion dragged him by his throat across the ground.

"Have any of them died?" Beladorion asked.

"No, my liege," answered Olthrion. "We've managed to take them all without killing them, though this one has murdered four of our men and several battalion soldiers."

"Yes, he is quite the warrior. Truly exquisite and precise. He would have made a remarkable Dead. Gather all the captured and take them into the mountain. Help the battalion tend to their wounded. Have some of our men gather the dragons and break them in."

"Right away, my liege."

"That was glorious," Ashur said, still covered in blood from his destructive rage. "I want more."

"And you shall have it, commander," said Beladorion. "I have here a man who has killed both your people and mine. A superb warrior. What shall we do with him?"

"I would say torture him, but I don't think he's got enough life left in him for that. Do you want to drink from him?"

"It won't do any good until the spell is broken. Besides, I don't think I'd like the taste of him."

"Then it sounds as if you've already made up your mind. I'm going to plan our next movement and interrogate some of the dragonborn. I'll start with the women. That should get their attention. If we leave now we should reach Arvall by—"

"We must wait. I know the exact time that we should arrive in the city and we can't come a moment before."

"Big plans?"

"Enormous."

Ashur left Beladorion with Oren. Beladorion kicked the proud warrior down and stood with his foot on his chest, grinning.

"It would appear you've reached the end," Beladorion said, slowly increasing the force behind his foot. "There is but one thing left to say to you as you take the sleep of your fathers. Fhealltóir Fola."

And with that Beladorion put all of his weight into one swift movement and crushed right through Oren's chest.

CHAPTER NINE

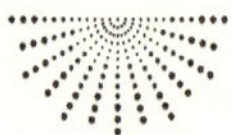

"Reports say the army is even closer. They're moving fast and at this rate they'll be here within two weeks," Lymir said.

"They're ahead of schedule now," said Raesh. "Even if all of Noelle came to our aid, they would never get here in time. We're going to have to work with the forces we have."

"That was a great speech you gave, Lymir," Andie said. "There's not much hope to go around these days, but what's left of it definitely spread through your speech. Also, I just noticed that you lost your accent. What happened?"

"I just figured that if I was going to lead the University and speak on its behalf it was probably best that I work on my oratory skills."

"Lymir, your leadership is going to help in the

next fortnight," Saeryn said. "I've been to the city just this morning and while the people are banding together to help each other, it's all they can do not to panic. I've been trying to resist the urge to take all the responsibility for this attack. If it weren't for me and my people no army would be marching on this city."

"If it weren't for the dragonborn it wouldn't be an army threatening the city, but the University," Raesh said. "And not just Arvall, but all of Noelle. People would still have hate and prejudice in their hearts. And anybody with dragon blood would be living in fear, just because of what they are. No matter what happens when that army arrives, the dragonborn saved us."

"I agree," said Lymir.

"Your words comfort me," Saeryn said. "But my personal feelings are of no matter just now. I've had the chance to look over Sarinda's report from her voyage. She wrote that a curious epidemic of Maeludrax disease was beginning in the True Isles. Thabes is almost completely shut down."

"That's the last thing we need," said Raesh. "The True Isles are supplying forty percent of our weapons and armor. Since when are there outbreaks in the True Isles? I thought their waters kept them disease free?"

"Precisely," Andie said. "It sounds like another trick of the army or the Church. If they can weaponize the red sand, then why not disease? The True Isles would be the perfect testing ground: a healthy population, secluded environment, almost nonexistent military presence. We can't let this go on. The True Isles are close enough to the Church that the priests would have known the isles were supplying us. Attacking them with this weapon makes perfect strategic sense. We have to help them."

Everyone nodded in agreement.

"I can leave this evening," Andie said. "I'll take a small party and we can be there by morning."

"And what will you do?" Raesh asked. "I'm all for helping them, but the cure for Maeludrax isn't something we can make or buy in Arvall. Taline had the last remaining vials in western Noelle, but they sent them across the continent last year to some poor villages. They haven't synthesized anymore and the process would take at least three days. What can you do?"

"I can give them my blood."

"What?"

"Saeryn and I have been reading over the grimoires. Before they were executed by the University, some of our third cycle ancestors were scientists. They were experimenting with the healing properties of our blood. Up until that point, they'd all been so scared of the University and the hunting that they suppressed their abilities and pretended to be normal. But they found their courage and ran countless experiments over a decade. Their work was cut short by their deaths, but before that they hadn't come across a single disease that their blood couldn't cure."

"Don't tell me the University killed a group of scientists who could have potentially eliminated disease from the world."

"They didn't just kill them. The scientists were based right here in Arvall on the mountainside. Remember that thing they taught in school? 'The Great Erosion of the Third Cycle?' The University bombed the mountain, killing all seventy scientists and causing the top thousand feet of Brie to slide down in an avalanche, which they diverted away from the University and instead let fall on the city. They ended up killing almost a thousand people that day."

"There's never an end to the evil, is there? But about your blood... even if that works, you can't give hundreds of people your blood."

"I don't need to. Not per se. I'll take a sample and amplify it by magic. Then I'll follow the instructions in the grimoire and distribute it. At least we can save some until the cure can be found and sent for. If the outbreak started days ago, there might not be many of them left."

"Go as swiftly as you can," Lymir said. "Our allies deserve to know that if they risk their lives for us we'll do the same for them."

"Okay. Saeryn, I'm sorry to ask this," Andie began, "but I need you to come with me. With Oren out of the city I won't have a dragon to ride. You up for an adventure?"

"Certainly."

Saeryn and Lymir left the apartment and Andie and Raesh were alone. Raesh stood and walked a bit, while Andie waited for him to say what she knew was on his mind.

"Okay, I'm not going to be that guy," he said. "The guy who said you can't go or starts worrying for your safety just because you want to go on a mission, no matter how insane. I won't doubt you or belittle you like that. You're the bravest, most powerful, most intelligent person I know. You're more capable than any of us. I'll just say be careful and that I'll be waiting for you when you get back."

She stood and went with him. She kissed him in a way she hoped thanked him for always doing the right thing, for always saying what needed to be said. He held her.

"I want you to do something for me," she said.

"What's that?"

"I want you to open something."

She turned and walked to the spare bedroom. She returned with a briefcase, but not just any briefcase: it was Marvo's. It was the briefcase Marvo kept his recipes in. Raesh's eyes widen when he saw it. Andie saw him struggling inside.

"Where did you find that?" Raesh asked. "I've been looking for it for months."

"I've been looking, too. Your father really hid this thing. I finally found it behind two secret compartments and a pretty tough safe. I wanted you to have it. And I want you to open it. Not for me, but because it's yours now and you should embrace it. Your father would have wanted you to have it. Marvo always bragged about how it would be yours someday. You don't have to cook anything or run the restaurant, but all of it is yours."

"It seems like someone else's life," he said, gently taking the case from her. "I've only been back to the restaurant a handful of times. It seems so small now, so old. There was a time when I looked forward to owning it. I had so many plans and ideas for how I was going to make it better and make it one of the greatest places in Arvall. And now I can't even..."

"You'll figure it out in your own time. There's no law that said you can't walk away from the restaurant if you want to. All of this is up to you and no one's going to judge you either way, as long as you face this. And the truth is... it *was* someone else's life."

Raesh stood there looking at the case for a few moments before he lowered his hands. He and Andie walked down the hall to the bedroom and he placed the briefcase in the closet. They lay down in the bed, in each other's arms, without saying a word, spending a few moments together before Andie began to start preparing.

A COUPLE HOURS LATER, Andie was stroking the head of Saeryn's dragon. It wasn't as big or as strong as her previous one, but Andie could tell this new dragon adored her just as much. He had claimed Saeryn as his own the moment his own rider had died. No matter how long Andie was around them or how many times she had ridden them, she's was always astounded. The creature responded to her touch, curling toward her and giving that deep rumbling purr that only dragons can make. Soon Saeryn exited the University and the two mounted up. They had four other riders alongside them. Andie double checked she had the right grimoire and the ingredients they would need for the spell—it was very old and very precise spellwork.

They flew in perfect chevron formation, high above the city and the people they had sworn to protect. With the dragon's great speed, it wasn't long before they were over the Spider Sea and it was a sight Andie would cherish for the rest of her life. She had never flown over the sea before and it looked even more beautiful from above. The soft light of the moon fell over the modest, coursing waves and created a new kind of perfect light. The silvery trench spiders were already near the surface, with their feather-shaped legs and dandelion bodies. It was devastatingly beautiful.

But even that incredible sight could only distract Andie for so long. She thought of the suffering Thabians in the True Isles. They had been a neutral party since the beginning of time. No one can remember when the Thabians fought a war or did anything other than help those in need. They were skilled fighters and excellent blacksmiths, but their supplying weapons to Arvall was only one of three recorded instances of them ever choosing sides in a conflict. While it made perfect sense to cut off the weapon supply, Andie couldn't believe anyone could be so evil as to infect the entire isles with that terrible disease—a disease that is extremely painful and fatal if not treated quickly. If they had known the Thabians would be attacked so heinously, they never would have set up the arrangement.

She was confident her blood and the blood of the other dragonborn would suffice as a cure; she'd checked and doublechecked and triplechecked the grimoire. She worried that they were too late. Maeludrax disease is a horrible sickness: it begins benignly enough, as most illnesses do, with a fever. But overnight the body becomes covered in black rashes so painful that even the blowing wind causes severe pain. Next the senses go: sight, sound, taste, touch, smell. By the second night the body's immune system is almost destroyed and only luck can save a person from dying from some common illness that normally wouldn't be an issue. By the third day the bleeding begins and the lungs begin to shut down. Some people, especially those with magic in their blood, can survive past that point if they're strong enough and are closely monitored. But most people didn't live longer than four days and no one lived past a week. Andie could hardly imagine it: an entire civilization dying.

The dragons flew all night since there was nowhere to stop and rest. They reached The True Isles when the morning was still black. All the isles were surrounded by the cerulean water that never darkens, not even when the sun goes down. It was an old and powerful magic that allowed the waters of the isles to touch the other seawater without mixing. They flew straight for Thabes, a beautiful city lit by the evanescent glow of its wildlife; every animal and insect in the True Isles glowed. It was never truly dark. The inhabitants had sworn off modern technology and instead lived off the land and in huts made from sand and clay. Andie had been overwhelmed with beautiful sights in her life and this was yet another one.

They landed on the beach and hurried toward the

only place in the city where the torches were still burning. Even before the dragons touched down on the beach, Andie could smell it: the scent of countless rotting corpses. They arrived at a large clearing and were halted by the shock. As far as the eye could see in front of them were bodies. Men, women, children, the elderly, even some of the larger animals that were mammals lay dead or dying. There were a few of the city's healers still moving around, helping where they could, but not nearly enough. Andie couldn't begin to count the people. As they moved forward again, Andie stepped in something and then pulled her foot back with a jerk. The sand was soaked in blood.

One of the healers saw them and came racing over. When he reached them, he began to speak faster than Andie could keep up with She realized he was speaking another language entirely. She tried to signal to him that she couldn't understand, but Saeryn grabbed the man and turned him toward her. She seemed to listen to him intently and then she turned to Andie.

"He said he welcomes us in the name of Alqwedelades, the god of him and his people. His begs for our help if we can offer any. He said all of the people who speak our tongue are dead or dying."

"How can you understand him?" Andie asked.

"He speaks High Thabian, a language older than

our people. It was once well-known across western and central Noelle and I learned it as a child."

The man began to talk again, his arms and hands were waving wildly in his begging gestures. Saeryn asked him something in his language and he responded.

"He said the sickness has been on them for nearly six days. Over half of the population is gone. I've asked him if there is any healer left who has magic and he said there is one woman beyond the trees, but she has come down with the illness just hours ago. She may still be strong enough. We must hurry."

Saeryn turned and said something else to the man. He motioned to her face and to Andie's and then said something back. Saeryn responded and the man dropped to his knees and began bowing over and over.

"What happened?" Andie asked. "What's he doing?"

"I think he's... worshipping us. I asked him to take us to the healer so that we could help them, but he said we needed masks. I told him we are dragonborn and don't get sick, and then he began to bow."

Saeryn leaned over and raised the man up. She spoke to him so soothingly that Andie was almost calmed herself. The man made a final half bow then began hurrying toward the trees, with the dragonborn following. When they reached the woman, they could see that she had the fever and a few small rashes, but was still able to walk and lend assistance. Saeryn spoke with her and the woman exhaled a sigh of relief.

"Okay, princess," Saeryn said. "Let us begin."

Andie got the grimoire and began following the instructions for the spell. She cut her hand and caught the blood in a bowl. She finished the preparation and then said the incantation. She drew the blood into a syringe and gave the woman a dose. They waited. It didn't take long before the woman's complexion improved and the rashes began to slowly recede.

"That's amazing," Andie said. "I read the grimoire, but I don't think I actually believed it would work until just this moment."

"There have always been tales about the blood of our people," Saeryn said. "It's nice to know that some of the good ones are true. I wonder that no one has exploited these properties before."

"According to the pages, our blood can cure most known diseases, under most circumstances, but it can't cure wounds. It can't cure serious medical conditions, so nothing neural, spinal, circulatory, or anything like that. It's powerful, but not all-powerful. Still pretty amazing."

Andie filled another syringe and gave the man a shot as well, to protect him.

"Do you think you can do the spell?" she asked Saeryn.

"Yes, it seems simple enough."

"Good. I have another mission I need to attend to. You and the other dragonborn will have to take care of these people. Teach her the spell."

"But where are you going?"

"To take back our destiny."

CHAPTER TEN

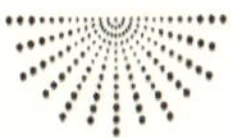

Andie left the group and took off through the woods. When she was far enough away that was sure no one could see her, she took out the journals. She had gotten them from Marcus before they left the University. She flipped to the page she was looking for and it didn't take long to find: the location of House Terpsichore's secret portal. She would've told Saeryn what she wanted, but she didn't trust that Saeryn would understand. It was simpler that way. The Thabians needed the blood of her people, but her people needed the portal. Andie closed the journal and began her trek through the forest.

Everything about the True Isles was unusual and contained, including its climate. No matter what the weather on the ocean was like, the skies were always warm and clear over the isles. The climate was perfect along the beaches and huts, but deeper inland it was that of a jungle. Hot, humid, heavy. The wildlife was exotic, and Andie couldn't finish being surprised by one creature before she came across the next. It was not difficult to make her way because the foliage there was gently controlled by the Thabians to be a perfect balance that provided shelter for the animals, but also made hunting easier. The glowing creatures lent plenty of light, almost too much, and while Andie made her way with ease she also worried about being seen. But worry was pointless. Most of the inhabitants were dead.

She walked for some time, her hand was level with her face and ready to cast at a moment's notice. She was not convinced some of the army didn't stay behind to make sure everyone died. But she saw no one. In fact, the closest she had come to other people was passing three mass burial sites where she couldn't even begin to count the dead. She'd cast a spell over her nose and mouth so that the stench of the dead didn't make her sick. Yet there was no spell for the sadness. There was nothing she could do to stop her tears when she saw the sight of all those bodies that would never live or love again. They were just more reasons that fueled her anger and determination.

The journal said the portal was hidden beneath a Wellensbard, a trap from the old days. Wellensbards were objects that created optical illusions that only dissolve once the riddle they represented had been solved. The journal gave the general location of the Wellensbard, but because the author feared other families finding the portal, there were no specific instructions. The journal didn't even give a hint. Andie arrived in the area and had no idea where to start.

"Great. Tease me with the location of an ancient portal that can be used to get rid of my entire race and then leave me hanging."

She walked back and forth over the area, which must have been fifty square meters. She checked tree trunks, both sides of the small creek that splits the area, and anything that looked like it could have been in the wrong place. But all she saw was trees, plants, and a perfect night sky. Nearly two hours passed as she wracked her brain and poured backwards and forwards through the passage in the journal. She hadn't missed anything in the pages. She decided to try something. She raised her hands over the ground and prepared.

"Solas revelati—"

She had only just begun the revealing spell when the entire fifty square meter area exploded in a cloud of dirt, rocks, and tree roots. Andie was blasted off her feet and into a tree trunk. Hard. The dragon blood healing began immediately, but she had broken some ribs and she could feel the blood trickling down the back of her neck from a cut on her scalp. She had to lie there for a moment to catch her breath and heal. She knew she should've been smarter; Wellensbards were notorious for being spell-proof and extremely dangerous if messed with. If Andie wasn't dragonborn, she would've been in serious trouble.

"Well, at least I know I'm in the right place," she said, sitting herself up against the base of a tree. "That hurt. That really hurt. But I've got to find this thing. There's no way we can find them all before that army gets here, but I can get this one. I just have to think. Come on, Andie. The journal doesn't give anything specific, but there must be some clue. House Terpsichore would never run the risk of its descendants not finding the portal. They thought they were the only family who had one. Think. What do you know about them..."

House Terpsichore had been the most jovial of the seven families. They were the most ambitious and energetic at the parties and loved to hold competitions and pageants. They were no richer or poorer than the other families, though they had as many secrets. The seal of their house had been two lovers in dance, wreathed in some other smaller details that Andie couldn't remember. Over the last thousand years, the family didn't seem to have changed at all. She still heard stories about the extravagant parties they threw in east central Noelle. But that was as much as Andie could remember, and though she'd read the entire journal front to back there was nothing in it that could help her. All she saw was their pageants and their seal.

"Wait," she said. "That's it."

Before she'd even completely healed she hurried to her feet and began to dance. She was not quite sure of where the precise spot was so she moved all around the area, dancing as best and as truly as she could to a beat she didn't hear. If anyone had walked up they might have thought she was losing her mind. She danced across the jungle floor. Finally, she saw the land around her begin to disintegrate. When the illusion was finally revealed, she had to move quickly to avoid falling in.

"Well, would you look at that..."

The portal looked exactly like the one in the University, except this one was half buried and turned itself off. The automatic activation must have been a final security measure for anyone who found it that shouldn't have. Andie ran her hand over the smooth surface. She'd never seen one inactive before. The face of the portal was smooth, almost too smooth. A hard surface with absolutely no friction. Andie couldn't even begin to fathom the magic that went in to creating it.

"One down. Six to go."

· · ·

BY THE TIME Andie made it back to the dragonborn, they'd already made considerable headway in healing the Thabians. Many of the bodies that were once lying prostrate were now sitting up. None were walking yet, but Andie figured the longer they were sick, the longer it would take them to heal. She was just glad it was working at all.

"Andie, where have you been?" Saeryn asked, looking half panicked. "You've been gone for hours. I almost sent people to look for you."

"I was sure you would after the explosion," Andie said sheepishly.

"I trust you're referring to the explosion that frightened us all to death. I almost went myself, but these poor people needed help. I trusted you to survive whatever it was and come back with a spectacular reason for your abandoning the mission, which, I feel it not inappropriate to add, was your idea. People are dying by the hundreds here and you're off exploring in the jungle. Disappearing, explosions, cryptic excuses. I expect more from the princess of our people. I have never been so disappointed with you."

Andie didn't want to admit it, but Saeryn's words almost cut her in half. Not once since she came out of the portal had Saeryn ever said anything like that to her. Andie could not have been more hurt if Saeryn physically tried to kill her. She simply stood there, weighing in her mind whether or not her excursion would be enough or if the truth will get her back in Saeryn's good graces. Regardless, the Queen of the dragonborn needed to know.

"I'm sorry, Saeryn. And I'm so grateful to all of you for helping to save these people. I know this was all my idea and that I took off without giving you a good explanation, but it was only because I didn't think you would understand and if you did I didn't think you would let me go."

"I think it's best you be honest with me now, Andie."

"I went searching for the portal. The one that's been hidden here for centuries. And I found it."

Saeryn and the other dragonborn turned their full attention to her and gawked. She had rarely, if ever, seen the Queen speechless. She took it as a good sign.

"House Terpsichore buried their portal here centuries ago and left a trail for their descendants, never knowing of course that it would be us, the dragonborn, who'd find it. I got the journal back from Professor Iceubes just before we left. When I finally got to the area, it took a little deductive reasoning, but I uncovered it. I'm not afraid to say I got lucky and the rest probably won't be so easy to unearth, but we're one step closer to controlling our destiny."

Saeryn continued to stare at Andie, almost as if she couldn't understand what she was being told. Andie stepped forward to take her hands.

"We shouldn't have to live in constant fear of these portals being used against us or anyone else. These things are incredibly dangerous and I don't trust them in anyone's hands but ours. I made arrangements for a ship to leave the port at Arvall and follow us here. It probably won't arrive for another day or two, but they can load the portal and get it back safely. Please tell me I've done a good thing."

Saeryn still couldn't speak, but she threw her arms around Andie and held her close. A weight fell off Andie's heart. But when Saeryn let go of her it was a severe face, not a relieved one, that faced Andie.

"You've done a superbly good thing, princess. But you need to remember who you are. You're one of us and nothing you undertake is undertaken alone. Trust your people. Trust me. And never, no matter how great the possibility of reward, abandon those in need. It is not our way. The portal had been buried and undisturbed for centuries, and I doubt a few more hours would have hurt it. I am so very proud of you for your continued efforts to protect our people. We all know you love us. But we are a strong, resilient people. And you must promise me that from now on you will put others first."

"I promise."

"Good. Now, we still have work. Let us work to save some more lives and then you can show me the portal of House Terpsichore."

They worked tirelessly for as long as they could without resting. Eventually, they had enough of the Thabian healers on their feet to continue the work. They gave as much blood as they could afford and then the Thabians fed them and let them drink from their private waters. The food replenished them, the water made them better than they'd ever been before. Andie could try for the rest of her life and never be able to describe the taste and effect of that water.

After Andie showed the portal to Saeryn and their dragonborn warriors, it was time to take off again. Saeryn insisted that the city would need them for the preparations and the citywide evacuation.

"I can't imagine the chaos of all those poor people clambering up the side of the mountain to seek shelter in the University. There's certainly enough room for them all. The University's rooms, tunnels, and corridors go deep into the mountain. But it will take the next two weeks just to get them all up there with only SKY 6."

"That's the beauty of having this portal," Andie said. "It can be used for transportation. Marcus has all the notes on how to control the portals and set them up. As soon as the boat comes and carries this portal back to Arvall, it'll speed everything up."

"Excellent news. I confess I'm also worried for Oren."

"He's the best warrior the dragonborn have. I'm sure he's just being thorough."

"Yes, but he should have returned by now. One day when you're Queen, you'll learn that your people are your children and your job is as much to worry for them as it is to love them."

"I don't know what kind of Queen I'll make. I don't think I'll ever be ready for that."

"Well, we dragonborn live long lives, but we are not immortal. One day I will pass on and you will be the new leader. In fact, I may even step down if I think you're ready. And I'll tell you a little secret."

"What's that?"

"No one is ever ready."

They smiled. They gathered their belongings and trudged through the jungle to the clearing. They said goodbye to the Thabians and had to work hard to keep them from bowing. They reached the sands of the shore and mounted their dragons, ready for the flight home. The sun had been up for hours and the sunlight had done them all good.

"Saeryn, wait," Andie said.

"Is something the matter?"

"Not exactly. Look, we're already out here, a full afternoon and evening's flight from home, why don't we just keep going?"

"To where?"

"Most of the portals are out of our reach, at least

for the time being. But we have more than enough time to fly to New Carthage and look for the portal of House Thalia. I know you want to get back to help, but there's nothing we can do back there other than train professors or stock food. There's plenty of people who can help with that. The Beautiful Dead, wherever they are and whatever they're doing, they seem to know more than we gave them credit for, and if they're as cunning as you suggest, they might even know about these portals. They and the Church have been one step ahead from the start."

"I don't know, Andic. The army has sped up its movements."

"Even if they ran nonstop we could still be back long before they arrive. I won't lie and say I'm sure of anything, but I trust you, Saeryn. I'm asking you to trust me."

"I've trusted you even when you didn't trust yourself. To New Carthage we go."

CHAPTER ELEVEN

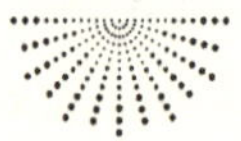

Raesh and Lymir sat in the meeting room, going over battle plans and supply lists again. Many of the other professors had left or busied themselves with some small correspondence on their laptops. Everybody was startled back to the room when a bloody man rushed in, breathing hard and barely able to stand.

"They've found us! We need help! Please, someone must help us!"

"What's wrong?" Raesh asked, catching the man as his legs gave out. "You're dragonborn. But you're hurt. Why aren't you healing?"

"The Dead have found us. They captured them."

"Captured who?"

"Everyone. Men, women, younglings, the old. And they can ride our dragons."

"Why can't you heal?" asked Lymir.

"Their weapons. I've never seen such blades. They have swords that can hurt us in ways I've never seen. They didn't kill us, but it would have been only too easy."

"What do they want? Money? Land? What?" Raesh asked.

"The only thing the Dead have ever wanted. Our blood."

"How many got away?"

"Only myself. Two others were with me, but the Dead mounted our dragons and took them."

"Where's Oren? Did he get captured? Have they hurt him?"

"Oren... Oren... My general..."

"Where is he?" Raesh asked again, desperate.

"He's dead."

TWO DAYS LATER, Andie and her party flew in over the walled city of New Carthage. The original Carthage had been completely washed away in a flood, six cycles previously. New Carthage was built upon the ruins of its predecessor, but, even all those years later, it had yet to be complete. It had been called the City of a Thousand Laws because of the bureaucratic red tape that constantly delayed the city's completion, including the writing and rewriting of countless laws, tax revisions, and an intricate maze of zoning permits that had yet to be sorted out.

The New Carthaginians were a friendly enough people, much like the Thabians, without the beauty or seaside resorts. New Carthage was an extremely secretive city, and one of the most attractive and baffling things about it was its collection of godhearts. Dehydrated hearts of an ancient race of beasts that used to roam the region. Godhearts were one of the most sought-after commodities in all of Noelle. They had no practical use, but, as time passed, they came to be bought and used as jewelry. Jewelry of a kind that most would never be able to see, let alone afford. A single ounce of godheart, properly preserved, could easily sell for a solid ten-pound gold bullion.

While Arvall was arguably the most influential and well-known city of Noelle, New Carthage was without doubt the richest. Andie and the dragonborn party landed just outside of the city, not wanting to frighten the citizens or cause a commotion. Their mission would be faster if they could maintain a degree of secrecy. They got the dragons to lie down behind a thick group of trees and bushes and then began their approach, carefully.

"Remind me," Saeryn said. "Where exactly do the New Carthaginians' loyalty lie?"

"No one's sure," Andie answered. "We've reached

out to them several times, but they've never reached a decision."

"What do you mean?"

"Well, apparently they take the whole democracy thing pretty seriously. The whole city votes on every major issue. Becoming our ally was a major issue. The vote wasn't heavy enough either way to make a firm decision and their city council didn't want to risk a move that could divide the city. The last I heard, they were conducting another vote and couldn't decide, but that was weeks ago. I'm pretty sure they're just ignoring us now."

"You said they voted before? Which way did they lean? More toward befriending us or more against us?"

"They wouldn't say."

They walked some distance before Saeryn stopped them and motioned for them all to hide. A trio of armed men marched by. Andie groaned audibly. There hadn't been any sorcerers born into New Carthage for years and so the city had to either hire people who had magic or hire people who use guns—the old-fashioned kind, not the terrible ones from the University. Andie was rather hoping security would be lax there, but they had just run into an armed, competent patrol before they'd even entered the city. That didn't bode well for what they'd find inside.

"Anyone who takes this long to come to a decision

about a move so critical to not just our, but all of Noelle's survival, can't be trusted," Saeryn said. "Everyone knows what lies horded beneath these streets."

"Godhearts," Andie replied. "I thought the same thing. They don't want to pick a side because they don't want to risk losing their precious treasure. These people are not our allies."

"Agreed."

"But how far does that go and what do we do if we get caught? There's a big difference between just not being our ally and actively being our enemy."

"I suppose we could never answer that sufficiently by ourselves. My suggestion would be to not get caught."

Andie turned to Saeryn and saw that she was smiling. Saeryn reached down into a pocket of her bag and pulled out something thin and soft. Craiceann.

"I haven't seen any of those in a while," Andie said, taking the one Saeryn handed her.

"I had a feeling you had other plans when we took off from Arvall," Saeryn said. "One of the many cliché maxims that prove true when you become a Queen: always be prepared."

"Especially when your princess is always up to something."

She and Saeryn put the gossamer masked on and waited while the magic of the craiceanns changed their entire appearance. They got a good look at each other so they wouldn't forget what the other looked like, and Saeryn instructed the dragonborn warriors to stay with the dragons and be ready to leave or come to their aid at a moment's notice. She and Andie began walking toward the city gates.

"I've spelled these to give us the darker skin and exotic habits of the New Carthaginians," Saeryn whispered. "We should pass for them quite easily. Once we are past the gate we'll be fine, but if they stop us here then the mission is over before it starts."

Andie gave a slight nod and continued smiling, as if Saeryn were telling a funny joke. They waited in line at the gate until it was their turn. The guard took a long, odd look at them, but eventually waved them past. But as he waved his watch fell and Saeryn bent over to pick it up. She handed it back to him.

"*Gaeree*," the guard said, putting the watch on again.

Before he looked up, Andie was already raising her hand to cast. She had no idea what language he was speaking and knew it was only a matter of seconds before he figured out they were the imposters. She was about to blast him away when Saeryn speaks.

"*Praegio*."

Saeryn turned from the guard and moved through the gate as if nothing had happened. A stunned Andie was left standing stock still until she realized that everything was okay. She took a few hurried steps to catch up with Saeryn.

"How many languages do you speak?" she asked.

"Quite a few. You will, too, one day. The leader of any people should always speak multiple tongues so as to show respect to other leaders and their people. Cities will deal with you much quicker when they realize you've taken the time to learn their language. Come."

The streets of New Carthage were much the same as the streets of any major city, only cleaner and more expensive. When you have a seemingly unlimited supply of godhearts—which couldn't be found anywhere else in Noelle—it seemed you could afford a more beautiful city. The people even seemed more beautiful, somehow. The market district was alive with shoppers and patrol guards, though the police presence was far less intimidating within the city walls. Andie thought hard about where the portal should be, trying to remember the exact instructions in the journal. She wanted to pull out the journal to doublecheck, but she didn't want to risk anyone seeing it.

She and Saeryn walked for some time. The journal said the portal was buried near the center of the city. Luckily, the never-ending construction of New Carthage was a huge tourist attraction in Noelle and there were sightseeing maps placed regularly. Andie and Saeryn stopped at one, then continued toward the center of the city. As they walked, Saeryn told Andie stories of her reign as Queen and some of the sacrifices she's had to make. She told Andie about the heartache and how the responsibility was severe when necessary, but also about the loyalty, the hope, the love.

It had been apparent to Andie for months that Saeryn had been grooming her to take the throne. She hadn't been too worried about it, because it would clearly be years before she was ready, but she did wonder about some things that she couldn't bring herself to broach with Saeryn, not the least of which was whether or not her relationship with Raesh was suitable. She hoped it was okay, because if not there was no way she'd ever ascend to the throne. For all she knew, she wouldn't be allowed to have relationships at all. Saeryn certainly didn't seem to have any love interests, not that that was an appropriate detail to bring up in casual conversation.

As they walked, Saeryn tapped Andie twice on the inside of her elbow. Andie tapped Saeryn back twice, then tapped her four times on the shoulder. All the gestures were quick, precise, and done with smiles. Saeryn gestured again and they turn right, into an alley. Andie bent down, pretending to tie Saeryn's shoe. They stayed that way until a man in a pea coat and white slacks turned into the alley, walking very deliberately. As soon as he was close, Saeryn stopped feigning ignorance and stuck him with a punch so hard and fast that even Andie leaped back. The man collapsed to his knees.

"I don't know what's more impressive. The languages or that," Andie said.

"You don't fight as many battles as I have and not pick up skills. Does he have any identification? Any papers at all?"

"No, there's nothing. Wait."

"What?"

"I… I think I recognize him."

Andie stared hard at the face, trying to place when and where she saw him. His pale grey eyes were rare and distinctive. The longer she looked at him, the closer she came to remembering.

"Hurry, Andie. I don't like the feeling of this alley. We should finish our mission and get back to the dragons as quickly as possible."

"Jasper Forlet," she said finally. "I took a class with him at the University, before everything happened. What's he doing here and why did he attack us?"

"I believe I can answer that."

Saeryn bent down and pulled at that top buttons of Jasper's shirt. It revealed battalion armor underneath.

"Great," Andie said. "Just what we need. Let's go."

They hid the unconscious body and returned to the street. No one seemed to have noticed. They relaxed. They walked for some time in silence because as they passed out of the market district the crowd thickened. Andie looked around her, trying to figure out why the crowd had become so dense. She grabbed hold of Saeryn and pulled her through until, at last, they reached the front.

"We must be near some major attraction," Andie said. "At least if anyone else is following us we can lose them in here. How did the battalion even find us?"

"They must have already been here. He was probably stationed outside of the city and saw us land before we changed our appearance. There's no telling what they were up to."

"Oh, I think I know exactly what they were up to and why the crowd is so big here. Look."

Andie pointed through some bystanders and Saeryn's gaze followed her finger. There was a massive hole in the center of the intersection. Nearby was a sign for tourists:

YOU ARE NOW STANDING ABOVE THE
LOCATION OF
THE SINGULARE AND UNFATHOMABLE
COLLECTION OF
THE GODHEARTS

OF THE CITY OF NEW CARTHAGE.
WELCOME.

"Well, that was dumb," Andie said. "Who puts a giant sign above the exact location of the world's largest collection of the rarest gems known to man?"

"The battalion, the Dead, and the Church could fund their war for a century with only a handful of what's down there."

"Yeah, and I'm betting they took more than a handful. We're never going to catch a break."

"Well, at least we can locate and secure the portal. The exact center of the city, correct?"

"You want to know what else is at the exact center of the city? This giant crime scene where the battalion stole the one thing this entire city is obsessed with. This place will be crawling with patrols and investigators for months."

Andie ran her hands through her hair, frustrated to be so close to the portal. It hurt. And it made her exceedingly angry.

"Be calm, princess. We'll get what we came for. I refuse to leave this city without it. First, we'll find somewhere to avoid suspicion until nightfall. Then we'll come back and I'm sure that two powerful, intelligent dragonborn of royal blood can find a way to get what we want."

. . .

Some hours later, night finally fell over New Carthage. The hole left by the battalion's heist was still uncovered and the godhearts below were exposed to the moonlight. The light of the crescent moon reflected off the jagged, unrefined surfaces of the godhearts in a dazzling, speckled pattern that danced across all the nearby buildings. By the time Andie and Saeryn returned, the city authorities had already pushed the lines four blocks back to keep away tourists and preserve the crime scene. Growing somewhat desperate, Andie tried out her feminine wiles on one of the patrol officers. Unfortunately, of the many gifts she had, flirting wasn't one of them. Saeryn couldn't help but laugh.

"It was a noble effort, princess. I'm sure if you were here in your true appearance we would have a different outcome."

Andie felt mortified, her cheeks tinging with a soft shade of rose. "I appreciate you trying to make me feel better. I might have another idea, though. Something my father taught me."

She took a breath and cast her spell. Everything around them slowed down.

Saeryn seemed shocked. She looked around herself at the passerby who appeared to barely be moving, his front foot suspended in mid-air as he stepped forward.

"This is incredible. Is this a variant of *Eitilt*?"

"I don't think so. It doesn't stop time, it just makes you move faster. A lot faster. Follow me."

Andie ran toward the massive hole and over the edge, Saeryn at her heels. They moved so fast they could run along the cavern walls, though the path was rough and slippery. They only just managed to make it to the ground when they hit a sort of wall and were knocked back. It took them a moment to catch their breath. The moment they were on their feet, they were surrounded by officers. Andie looked over at Saeryn. They'd been caught in a trap, which was one reason Andie never used the speed spell. It was great for some instances, except when defenses had already been put in place. It was too easy to protect against.

"Hands up, thief," an officer yelled, leveling his gun on them.

Several other guns came up as well, and the cavern filled with the sound of clicks as nearly thirty hammers were cocked.

"Actual firearms," Andie said. "A little outdated, don't you think?"

"Still kills just fine. We knew you'd come back. Nobody who gets their hands on one of these ever loses the taste for it and you got your hands on a lot of these. Where's your stash? Is this all of your gang?"

"There's been a misunderstanding," Saeryn tried to explain. "I realize we are here under suspicious circumstances—"

"You mean you were caught trying to sneak in using magic?"

"Yes, but we are no thieves. We came here in search of something else. Something of far greater value to us than godhearts. What we seek has the power to save or destroy, and we have no need of your precious stones."

"What is it you're looking for? Huh? Who are your people? You better start giving me some answers or the city council's going to have you in front of a high judge in the morning."

Saeryn seemed at a loss. The look on her face matched Andie's thinking. They'd been caught. The officer turned to Andie.

"How about you?" he asked. "Do you speak?"

"Yeah, I speak."

"Then start talking. Who are you and what do you want here?"

"Unfortunately for you, your city is indecisive. Which means I don't know which side you're on. Which means I can't tell you anything because it could become a diplomatic nightmare if you know who we really are and what we're after. That's all just a long way of saying that this is really going to hurt."

CHAPTER TWELVE

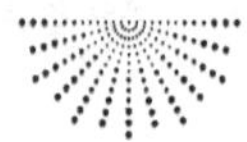

ANDIE STRUCK FIRST, HITTING THE TWO NEAREST officers with a bolt of lightning that didn't kill them, but threw them backward into the small mountain of godhearts. Saeryn went next, removing her scarf in an awesome flash of speed and magic, the fabric suddenly a solid yet flexible steel. She whipped it back and forth like a double-edged sword, taking out officers all around. On the other side, Andie got in close for hand to hand combat, taking the officers down without seriously injuring them. They were stronger than she was, but she was faster by far and had been trained by several of the greatest fighters in Noelle. In no time at all, she and Saeryn had the authorities put down. But they knew they don't have much time.

"Which way?" Saeryn asked.

Andie quickly pulled out the journal and opened it to the marked page. Once again, there wasn't much to go on, just like back in the True Isles. Andie was forced to think of everything she could remember about House Thalia. Unfortunately, she remembered even less about this house than she did the last. She turned to Saeryn.

"Tell me everything you know about House Thalia."

"Searching for the portal?"

It was not Saeryn who had spoken, but another female voice behind them. Andie turned and saw a police officer aiming a gun at them. The woman must have just arrived. Saeryn moved to pull her scarf off again, but Andie was quicker. She shot magic into her legs and launched herself at the woman. They both slammed into the ground. Saeryn rushed forward to help, but suddenly stopped. Andie got to her feet and looked over, but Saeryn didn't seem to see her. Andie gestured to her, but did not get a response. Saeryn was pacing and seems to be shouting, but Andie couldn't hear her. Then Andie looked over to the woman, who had her hand up, casting a spell.

"You first, then her," the woman said, practically snarling

"That's impossible," Andie said. "The police in New Carthage don't have magic. Who are you?"

"An imposter like you. The difference is I'm

leaving here alive." Faster than Andie thought anyone could cast, the woman sent out a spell that sucked up all the oxygen around them. Andie fell to her knees, feeling her lungs collapse against themselves. But she had enough strength to raise the earth around the woman and trap her arms. Barely. Andie motioned with her weak hands as she suffocated, and the woman was pulled over and down, the earth around her arms remerging with the ground and trapping the woman up to her chest. Andie broke the spell and breathed a painful, ragged breath, but the woman cracked the ground and got up again. They traded spells, Andie hitting her with a ball of purple fire and being hit with a flurry of cuts from invisible knives in return.

The woman conjured a pair of long daggers made of the very wind and rushed in. Andie used every bit of her considerable training to avoid her; the woman was superb with the daggers, as if it was a dance or a work of art. Andie managed to land a few hits, but took just as many. The woman finally managed to cut Andie on her arm and the force of the wind dagger slicing her arm spun Andie on her feet. Furious, Andie reached up to her face and pulled the craiceann off, revealing her true face and body. She drew the sword from her hip and took a stance, prepared to end this.

"Andie?"

There was a slight delay while Andie realized that the woman had called her name.

"Who are you?" she asked. "How do you know my name?"

"I didn't think I'd ever see you again."

Andie stared into the face of the woman, noting her eyes, mouth, hair, build, but had absolutely no idea who was standing in front of her. The woman twisted her arm through the air and removed the spell blocking Saeryn. As soon as she could hear and see them again, Saeryn spelled her scarf and moved to attack the woman.

"Wait!" Andie called.

She moved to Saeryn and pulled her craiceann off as well, revealing the Queen of the dragonborn in all her glory. The woman's eyes went wide as she saw the face. She knelt and lowered her head.

"Forgive me, your grace," she said. "I would never have attacked if I'd known who you were. I'm sorry to tell you that you're too late. The portal is gone. I came looking for it, too, but it was already gone when I arrived. I came to claim it for you, I promise."

"Rise, stranger," Saeryn said. "I am not opposed to forgiving you if you will say how you know us and who you are."

"It's me," the woman said, with an expression not far from pleading.

The woman stood and her hand moved to her face.

She pulled off a thin mask and the face she was wearing slid away. Another craiceann. And the face revealed was one that neither Andie nor Saeryn could believe. Andie can only manage one word.

"No."

Blackness.

"FHEALLTÓIR FOLA."

Beladorion stood over one of the dragonborn warriors, only just finishing beating the man until he almost died. Now the leader of the Dead waited for the dragon blood to kick in.

"I've always loved beating you blood traitors. As long as I don't kill you, the dragon blood heals you and we can begin again. But enough for today. I'll say one thing for you, you're not easy to break."

Beladorion left the man in a pool of his own blood and moved toward the front of camp. Along his way, he passed the rows and rows of dragonborn in cages. The dragonborn were a dignified people; they neither screamed nor pleaded. They were all confident their Queen and princess would find them and exact terrible vengeance. Beladorion locked his eyes on Ashur, who was doing some interrogating of his own. Although he was almost a hundred meters away, Beladorion could see and hear Ashur as if they were standing next to each other. He could smell the sweat of the dragonborn Ashur was beating. His senses and the senses of his people were unimaginable. Beladorion rushed forward and in seconds stood between Ashur and his victim.

"Commander," he said. "I'd like to go over our plan once more. I assure you, you'll be able to return to your plaything momentarily."

Beladorion headed to the front of the army. Most of the battalion soldiers and almost all of the Beautiful Dead were there, except those Beladorion dispatched with a special purpose. There may not have been a single army throughout all of time who could have stood against this force. Ashur followed Beladorion until they reached a small clearing.

"Is this supposed to be private?" Ashur asked. "No disrespect, but you and your people can hear across valleys. I don't really see what a few meters is going to do."

"I didn't bring you hear for privacy. I don't keep secrets from people. The only leaders who keep secrets from their own kind are greedy, cruel little cowards who wish they were gods. I brought you here to show you this."

Beladorion bent forward and grabbed the end of an enormous sheet and pulled. Ashur looked as if he'd seen a ghost. He experienced fear for the first time in a long while. He took several steps back.

"What is that?"

"You know very well what it is," Beladorion said, completely calm.

"How did you get it?"

"The same way I get anything. Patience and power."

"It shouldn't be here. That should be in Leabharlann."

"No, commander. This isn't the one you knew before. This is the portal of House Erato, buried for centuries under the abandoned city of Raven Deep. The one you knew is still in your library in the mountain Brie."

"There's more than one?"

"There are eight. One in your university, this one, and six more, each hidden by one of the founding families. I had some of my Dead excavate the portal of House Thalia in New Carthage some months ago. It's now with the army marching on Arvall. They'll set it up somewhere before they reach Gordric's Pain."

"And they'll be able to walk right into the University," Ashur said, beginning to understand. "The University and the city won't know what hit them. I'm starting to believe you're as cunning as you keep saying you are."

"Indeed. I doubt if anyone knows these portals still exist. I don't even think the descendants have a clue. When the times is right you and I will lead our army here to Arvall as well. So now I've proven again how useful I can be. And what do you offer?"

"I have agents in the University and the city. It's amazing how easy it is to buy some people's loyalty. All it took was the promise of a few godhearts. Speaking of New Carthage, my men should be done stealing their precious stones by now."

"I see you're no stranger to intricate webs."

"Not at all. I also have politicians and diplomats in my pockets. Hundreds of them. We've worked hard to turn as many as we can in eastern and central Noelle. After you convinced the Chancellor to kill those eight hundred ambassadors and heads of state at the Winter Festival, there was a chaotic scramble to fill those seats. We got our people into most of them. Their loyalty, if you can call it that, is contingent on our winning this war. If we lose, they won't back us and they won't risk moving against the dragonborn on their own. But if we win we'll have their support, their resources, and their influence. If that's not enough for you, I've been in touch with the descendants of the founding family since I first started my training under the Chancellor. Their hatred for the dragonborn has never wavered. If we win Arvall, they can help us win and control everything. They've also already begun a plan to destroy the Church. And I mean literally destroy that massive eyesore. And who can forget the icons? Millions of people all over western Noelle have gone to the University in Arvall and all have been given an icon. I know the magic that can command those icons to kill their hosts. It will take the entire battalion and all the power we can muster, but imagine: millions dead in an instant if they challenge us."

Ashur relaxed against the trunk of a tree and grinned at Beladorion, completely satisfied with his work.

"So there it is," he said. "You offer me a dragon-free Arvall and I offer you all of Noelle. Is that enough for you?"

"Yes, commander. That will do just fine."

CHAPTER THIRTEEN

"WE WEREN'T PREPARED FOR THIS," SAID RAESH, pacing the floor of lecture room 594.

"We could never have been prepared for this," Sarinda said.

Lymir sat beside her, thinking, as he had been since the warrior showed up. He hadn't said much in the two days since, but seemed lost in his own shock and confusion.

"When Saeryn and Andie told me about the Beautiful Dead, they said nothing about what they were capable of," Raesh continued. "And now they're not even here to help. They're off on some secret mission. We don't even know if they're okay."

"But we do know that the dragonborn need help," Sarinda said. "We have to send somebody, anybody. I'll go. I'll lead a team across the—"

"Sarinda, even if I wanted to, I couldn't send you. The trip takes roughly a day and a half by dragon. Since none of us can even ride dragons and there's no transport in the city that can get us there fast enough, it makes no sense to go. We can't send more dragonborn because we need them here for the war and whatever these Dead have, it's strong enough to stop the dragon blood healing. It's been two days and Sven still hasn't completely healed from his wounds. I don't want to say this, but I have to: any dragonborn captured by the Dead are on their own until Andie and Saeryn get back and we win this war."

"And then I'll be on the fastest transport I can find to cut some Dead legs off."

"I'll be right behind you."

"Okay," she said, shifting in her seat. "If the Dead are capturing them instead of killing them, then they obviously have plans for them. They should be safe for now, at least until this mysterious spell is broken. I just radioed the ship before I came here and apparently Andie arranged for it to go out to the True Isles and bring something back."

"Bring what back?"

"You're not going to believe it, but... a portal. I guess history is wrong again. There was one buried in the jungle that Andie found. I'm guessing there are probably more and that's where Andie and Saeryn are. I want them here as badly as you do, but if they're out finding portals I have to say that's way more important than sitting on their thumbs all day and night."

"Yeah, and if Marcus can operate those portals as well as he said he can then we can get people in here that much faster. We need to get as many inside these walls as we can, as quickly as we can. They'll be safe here."

"We'll have him meet the captain at the harbor and get people organized. But we also need to focus on getting people into the bunkers throughout the city. I think we're all safest here, but something just doesn't sit right with me about gathering everybody into one place. If by some chance the enemy *did* get into the University, the people of Arvall would be sitting ducks."

She stood and looked over at Lymir, waiting for him to speak. He returned her glance, then went back to staring into the middle distance. She turned back to Raesh.

"Well," she said. "Besides shelter I think we've got everything covered. We're as stocked as we can be with food and supplies, and the captain's also bringing the next loads of weapons and armor from the True Isles. I'll head back up to the summit and help with the training. It's just a waiting game now."

Sarinda left, touching Raesh on the shoulder as she went. Raesh stayed a while longer, hoping to get a conversation going with Lymir, but that effort bore no fruit. Soon enough he left, hoping sometime soon Lymir would be ready to return to his role. They might not have much time left.

Raesh went up to his apartment to pack a bag. When he was ready he took SKY1, then SKY 6, then the city shuttle train, then the crossland train, then the Sud, and then finally a cab, which dropped him off in front of the largest hospital in Taline. On the seventy-seventh floor, he had to go through a security checkpoint, an added measure to protect one of the most important people to him in the world. When he finally reached the room, Alecia was just finishing changing the drip.

"Raesh, hi," she said.

"Hey, Alecia. Any change today?"

"Well, for a moment earlier we thought so. There was a spike in brain activity and heart rate increased unusually, but she went back down. It was probably just a reaction to the drip. The doctor changed the medicine and dosing recently. Sorry, sweetheart."

"It's okay," he said, sitting in a chair beside the bed. "But I guess I have to ask: are you sure it was just a reaction?"

"Oh, I wish it were something more. You know, for a moment there I almost thought she was going to wake up. Her eyes. I could have sworn they were fluttering. Never mind. I'll leave you two alone. Goodnight."

"Goodnight."

Raesh settled in next to Carmen and changed her old flowers for the new ones he'd brought. He couldn't help thinking she looked so peaceful, so calm. It almost seemed like waking would be the real punishment. A part of him hoped that she wouldn't open her eyes for a while yet. He wanted her to wake to a new world, one where the war was over and everything that had been ruined had been rebuilt.

"Do you know what this is?" he asked her as he pulled a book from his bag. "This is one of my books. You've been begging me to let you read them forever. But I want you to know I didn't keep them from you because I didn't trust you. I just didn't think they were any good. But I'll let you decide for yourself. Before we get started, I don't know if you know this or not, but Andie and I are together. Together together. I know, it took us long enough. You can stop laughing now. She's not here tonight. She's off... being Andie. Sometimes I want to be mad her, but how can I? Her courage, her drive, her selflessness are all reasons why I love her. No, I haven't told her. Yes, I plan to as soon as I see her again. No one asked for your opinion, thank you very much.

"I love you, you know. And I miss you. You and your inappropriate, embarrassing jokes. We all miss you. But don't wake up yet. Not tonight. Wait a little while longer until Andie and I can fix this world for you, make it safe and beautiful for you again. You've been through so much, we all have. I just want to protect you. One more thing: we found more portals. Seriously. Yeah, I know... those things freak me out, too..."

Raesh began to read from his book. There were fifteen council fighters in the hall outside, but they didn't make a single sound, and, as he read, Raesh began to forget the world. For as long as he read it was just him and Carmen. He read until he couldn't keep his eyes open anymore. He closed the book and placed it back in his bag. He leaned forward and lay his head on top of his arms, right next to Carmen and fell asleep.

Sometime later, a hand moved through his hair. At first, he didn't respond.

"Raesh?"

The hand continued to move through his hair. Raesh began to stir.

"Raesh? Is that you?"

The voice and the hand combined finally brought him to the point of waking. Raesh yawned and looked around, blinking his eyes to bat away the blurriness. Finally, he looked at the face, the smile that was weak but familiar, the hand resting on his face. He couldn't believe it, even as he looked at her.

"Carmen?"

BACK IN THE UNIVERSITY, the portal was still open. Though Professor Iceubes now knew how to operate it, he'd been asked not to. No one wanted to do anything to it until Saeryn and Andie returned.

Just then the surface of the portal began to move, but the captain hadn't pulled into the dock yet and Marcus was still on SKY 6 on the mountainside. From the pretty, frictionless face of this device rose a man in robes. Five more followed him. In a perfect, slow-moving line the men walked forward from the Archives into the gargantuan space of Leabharlann.

They wandered, looking about them and examining books, but always moving steadily and deliberately toward the door. Without warning, those doors opened and all of the men stopped in their tracks. Two professors stood in the doorway, looking at the men in total bafflement. One of the robed men glided gracefully forward to just within a few feet of the professors. The professors took the stances they learned while training on the summit. But they were new recruits and had only had a couple classes. They came from money and privilege, and had never fought before. The robed man raised his hands beside him and held still. The professors were just about to attack when a great cloud of red sand bursts from his robe and engulfed the two professors. They didn't even have time to scream.

Once they were dead, the robed man, the priest, returned to his fellows, who gathered in the middle of the great library. They formed their line and moved just as slowly and deliberately back down to the portal. They leaned forward over the surface.

"It..."

"Seems..."

"The..."

"Way..."

"Is...

"Clear."

CHAPTER FOURTEEN

It was the next morning when Andie woke. She was lying in a room she didn't recognize. Outside the window, she saw they were still in New Carthage, though now they were on the other side of the city. She sat up slowly, her head was clear and at the same time heavy. She still didn't understand how dragonborn can be self-healing, but still faint.

"Be easy, princess. We're all safe."

At the sound of Saeryn's voice Andie turned to see her sitting on the next bed, smiling.

"I have to thank you for your fainting spell. If it hadn't been for that, I might never have had the experience of staying in a hotel. It's quite lovely.

"Was she real?"

"Yes. She is very real, Andie."

"Where is she?"

"You mean me?"

Just after her voice came around the corner, so did she. Andie needed a moment to make sure she wasn't dreaming and then she'd rush toward the girl she's missed so much. They threw their arms around each other.

"Yara," Andie whispered.

Andie hugged Yara as tight as Yara was hugging her. Saeryn watched from the bed.

"I thought you were dead," Andie said. "I saw you... I saw you..."

"You saw me carried away by a dragon. In its teeth, admittedly, but not dead. Although it did hurt. A lot."

"Wait, but then..." Andie paused, trying to remember her facts correctly. "When I learned the truth far later, Oren said he sent you through a time curse. Through the portal back to his time."

Yara smiled. "And he did, only it didn't work. He sent me back to a time somewhere between his own and ours, if I'm not mistaken. Only, something happened as soon as I arrived. The magic reversed and I was pulled back into our own world. I don't think anyone noticed, so I ran."

"I don't understand." Andie ran her hands through her hair, staring at her friend.

"Andie, it was the most beautiful place. And I suspect it might come in handy. I don't know how, or when. But just in case it helps…" Yara cast a strange and beautiful spell before the others, lifting her hands before her and chanting a short incantation. A shimmering image appeared before her and Andie and Saeryn both gasped in wonder. "This is what the spell in the portal looked like when Oren sent me through. If you can match this, we might be able to retrace my steps."

"Why would we ever do that?" Andie was incredulous, unable to take her eyes off the shimmering magic before her.

Yara dropped her hands and the image disappeared. "I don't know Andie, I hope we never will."

Andie sighed and rubbed her eyes. "Okay, that's something. But back to what's important, Yara. Everyone thought you were a traitor. I thought you were a traitor. They were going to execute you."

"And they probably would have. They'd only been on the mountain for a little while. They hadn't even built a real prison yet, so I just waited until I was alone. Then I ran. I ran for days, as far as I could go. I didn't stop until I reached the mine cities in the north. I collapsed next to a mountain of coal and I didn't think I'd ever wake up again. But a family found me there and took me in. They cleaned me up, fed me, nursed me, and let me stay with them as long as I wanted. I spent the next few days trying to figure out what I should do. I knew I couldn't go back to the Hot Salts or even to Arvall because all of you thought I was a traitor and the minute I showed my face I'd be dead."

"But why didn't you say something? When we were there on the beach and all of us accused you... when I accused you. You could've convinced us—"

"No, I couldn't have. The setup was pretty convincing and if I hadn't been in this body I would've thought I'd done it, too. And to be honest, I felt that I deserved punishment. I knew something was off about Marvo. You and Raesh had known him longer and had more of a connection with him, but you were blinded because you both loved him. I was working side by side with him those last few days and I knew, I *knew* something wasn't right, but I didn't say anything because I had no tangible proof and tensions were high enough as it was. I could see in your eyes every time you came around me you were growing more and more suspicious, and I wasn't exactly a ray of sunshine myself. I should've just knocked him out, hexed him, anything. I might've saved his life. All their lives. By the time we were standing there on that beach I was ready to die for having let things go on and turn the way they did."

"What changed your mind?"

"When they dropped me on the precipice, I started thinking. If the Chancellor had tapped into that kind of power, he had to be working with someone even more dangerous than he was. Myamar Mharú was cruel, but he was never that clever. But almost overnight he'd become a master manipulator and the leader of a vast battalion. It just didn't add up. I knew that you were focused on saving the dragonborn and taking down the University, and you didn't have the time or peace to notice that the Chancellor was a puppet master who had strings himself. That's when I knew I had to live.

"After the family got me on my feet again and I'd made up my mind to figure out who was behind the Chancellor's rise to power, I headed east. I tried to visit the village where I was born, but it was gone. Disease killed most of them, and the rest just left. It was totally abandoned. My journey also led me to the city I lived in when I ran away from home. It was a disaster, too, writhing with crime and corruption. A cesspool of evil. Finally, I ended up on the eastern coast of Noelle staring into the Divided Ocean. I had no leads, no allies, and no resources. So, I did the thing I swore I'd never do again. I stole. It's not something I'm proud of, but I still had the skillset and it save my life. Within two weeks I'd accumulated some considerable assets and disguised myself. Another week and I was having lunch with the affluent and leveraging the police. By the end of a month I achieved my goal and was invited."

"Invited to what?" Andie asked.

"To a ball given by House Polyhymnia," Saeryn said.

"How did you know?" asked Yara.

"When you were unpacking your bag, I saw a Braided Bangle, a common gift to those who get in close with the family. You must have quite the skillset, indeed."

"Admittedly. At the ball, I managed to ingratiate myself. It seems as long as you have money and a pretty face no one's interested in how you got where you are. Of course, the host family wasn't concerned with my past because they already assume they're better than everyone. I flattered, complimented, and lied. Before long I was sitting beside a group of the most recent generation of descendants. I plied them with champagne, no difficult task, and guided the conversation where I wanted it to go.

"It was incredibly disappointing at first. They were just complaining about how their family had fallen in stature and how they hoped the dragonborn would be hunted and killed before the year was out. I was about to leave when I decided to see what more they had to say on the dragonborn. That was the key. Soon they were telling me all about the horrors their family had committed against the dragonborn, bragging about it. They said the dragonborn were a cursed people even before the University began hunting them. They said their parents used to tell them stories about another group who were descended from the dragons and how that other group hated the dragonborn so much that they wanted to capture them and drink their blood. They said these other dragon descendants had helped the University in its hunt for dragonborn. I thought maybe they were just myths at first, but then one of them, Bonhaus, told me he'd been interested enough to do some digging around. He found out that the stories were more than just bedtime tales. They were actual history. That other group was known as—"

"The Beautiful Dead," Andie finished.

"So then it's true," Saeryn said. "We always suspected that they had a hand in helping the University destroy us. The University had never been anything but arrogant and incompetent. There was no possibility of them figuring out our weaknesses and being able to track us across the land on their own. It was the Dead helping them all along."

"So you've heard of them?" Yara asked.

"More than that," Andie said. "They're marching on Arvall and the University right now. They'll be there in less than two weeks. And Ash's battalion is coming, too."

"That doesn't surprise me. Bonhaus also told me his family and all the other founding families had recently been contacted by the battalion. He said that soldiers were stashed across Noelle and they were all coming together. The battalion wanted the support of the founding families and they got it. After that night, I started following the battalion."

"How did you catch their trail? We've been trying to find them for months."

"I didn't do it on my own. Bonhaus put me in touch with them. I followed them, picked a few of them off as I went, but I mostly just gathered information. I had enough money to afford a network of spies and there is hardly a police organization on the east coast of Noelle that can't be bought for the right price. It wasn't long before I realized the battalion were trying to contact the Dead. I knew that if they joined forces it would be catastrophic. I tried to stop it, but I could never figure out where the meeting was supposed to take place.

"But, like any sprawling and completely depraved organization, the Dead couldn't keep as lowkey and they wanted. There are only so many cookie jars a hand can reach into before people start asking questions and keeping track. I checked in with Bonhaus and he'd heard the same rumors. Someone was looking for something that belonged to his family, something House Polyhymnia wasn't supposed to have. Within a week there was a break-in at their mansion by a man and woman stronger and faster than was humanly possible. They tore the place apart, but didn't find what they were looking for. Because I already had it."

"What was it?

"A portal. The ancestors of House Polyhymnia hid one for themselves, right underneath their mansion. Bonhaus told me his grandfather had always filled them with stories about how they had a magical device more powerful than all the sorcerers of the world combined and that it was buried right under their feet. Assuming that story was as true as the others turned out to be, I got there first. It was too big for me to move by myself so I spelled it, just like I did Saeryn last night."

"So, it's still there," Andie said, impressed. "It's just invisible. The Dead must have been standing right on top of it and not even noticed."

"Exactly."

"Wait, I understand now. We were under the impression that the families had forgotten about the portals and the secrets of their ancestors, but they haven't. At least not entirely. They keep the secrets and histories alive in oral tradition, telling the story to generation after generation, only they don't know the stories are real. I can't believe it... these people are sitting on the biggest secrets in all of Noelle and they don't even know it!"

"I figured the same thing. I used Bonhaus and his family to get in with House Erato, but by the time I finally fell into their secrets and tracked their portal to Raven Deep, the Dead had already beat me there. But that didn't stop me. There was only one more house within range of where I was. House Clio in east central Noelle. But even Bonhaus couldn't get me in with them. House Clio has become sequestered from the other founding families and won't have anything to do with them. I had to go there and try to charm them on my own, but that failed miserably. So, I broke in.

"After fighting side by side with you and the council fighters against the University, a little personal security was no problem for me. I made my way inside, but I had no way of knowing where the portal was or if it was even on the property. I snuck into the master bedroom and spelled the wife so that she wouldn't wake. Then I sound proofed the room. I'll spare you the distasteful details, but let's just say the husband and I had a very frank conversation that he didn't like very much. He told me all the stories he'd been told as a child, one in particular about a magic doorway that was supposedly buried on the family's forest estate two hundred kilometers north.

"I got there as fast as I could. The estate was just coming in sight when I started to see trees falling. As I got closer I could hardly believe my eyes: there was a man and woman there knocking the trees down with their bare hands, like the trunks with nothing but foam. I figured they were Dead. I was lucky enough to take the man out by catching him by surprise with a strong spell, but the woman wasn't so easy. I can hardly even begin to describe the way she moved. Strong, agile, so fast I couldn't even keep up with her. She nearly killed me. I kept trying to defend myself and she would dash by me in a flash and send me flying. Finally, I was able to trap her and then get her still long enough to get in close with my wind daggers. I'd don't like the idea of ever facing one of them again."

"Don't worry," Saeryn said. "When the time comes it will be the dragonborn who face them. This has been a long time coming."

"Fortunately, she and the other one had already done most of the work. Before I snuck up on them, I let them clear the way and dig up the ground. Less work for me. That time I was prepared. I'd paid some people I could trust to keep quiet to move the portal. Now it's beside the other one under the mansion of House Polyhymnia."

"Is that safe?" Andie asked. "If they figure out that the stories are true they'll search for their portal. And when they go under their house and find not one, but two portals, I don't think they're going to be too shy about using them. We have to go get them. Now."

"They're safe, Andie."

"How can you think that?"

"Because Bonhaus and I wiped the memories of all of his family."

"Bonhaus and you? You honestly think you can trust this guy? Yara..."

"He's in love with me. I kind of... manipulated him. I had no choice. I needed someone on the inside, someone I could trust."

Andie just hugged Yara. Yara cautiously put her arms around her, too. By the bed, Saeryn stood, looking at Yara intently. Saeryn walked around the end of the bed, never taking her eyes off Yara, who looked back at her over Andie's shoulder.

"Everything you've done," Andie said, still holding her friend. "It must have been hard."

"You have no idea," Yara said.

"Back and forth across Noelle, taking on the Dead, giving up everything for this cause. And then having to endure a son of a founding family. I'm so sorry."

"Andie, there's something you should know. In the interest of being totally honest."

"Yes, I thought so," said Saeryn.

As Andie released Yara, Saeryn came nearer and placed her hand on Yara's shoulder.

"I can see it on you," Saeryn said. "I wonder if the best thing might be to leave the subject as it is for now. I'm sure we'll have ample time to discuss it later. Perhaps now it is most prudent to leave the city and rejoin our party on the outskirts of New Carthage."

"Leave what subject?" Andie asked. "What aren't you telling me, Yara?"

"Bonhaus. We worked side by side for so long and I was so... alone. I was doing it all by myself and then something happened. Between us. And I fell in love with him, too."

Andie took several steps back, looking both disgusted and horrified. Saeryn moved to touch her, but Andie shook her off. She advanced on Yara so menacingly that Yara took a step back in surprise.

"You fell in love with him?" Andie asked. "With a member of House Polyhymnia? One of the seven families who have been hunting and killing my people for centuries? Are you serious?"

"Andie, you don't know what it was like out there!" Yara countered. "I was all alone and I missed my friends, my city. I missed you! It was my own fault that I was out there, but when I needed someone Bonhaus was there. He gave me the information that helped me track the battalion and find both of the portals."

"He's one of *them*!"

"He went against his own family for me! For all of us! For you! He doesn't believe what they believe and he's never killed a dragonborn all his life. He's never even met one."

"He has the blood of killers and liars! It's in his blood, he's poisonous! They're all poisonous!"

"Andie, I would think you of all people would be the last one to judge someone because of what's in their blood."

"I don't care!"

"You act as if evil can be inherited like dragon blood. That's not the way it works, Andie, and I think you know that. I understand this is hard for you and I know that if I were in your shoes I'd be judging me, too, but I need you to hear me out. Yes, I was the one who stole, traveled, fought, infiltrated, manipulated, bought, bribed, and climbed my way to what I needed for you and for Arvall. But the information behind all of that comes from Bonhaus. He was the one who introduced me to important people and helped me get in places. He was the one who put countless hours into research over the last few months. He was the one who stitched me up after the Dead woman almost killed me. He kept me going. I know what he is and what he comes from, but that's not who he is or who he wants to be. You don't know him, I get it. Don't trust him, trust me."

Andie couldn't even bring herself to look at Yara. She spoke to the wall.

"Yara, I cant... I... I can't even begin to tell you how much I missed you. When we finally found out the truth, every one of us was devastated. I've cried myself to sleep thinking of you and not a day has gone by when letting you get taken by that dragon hasn't been the biggest regret of my life. But you need to understand that I'm not okay with this. I can't be okay with this. You're telling me that you fell in love with a man who is a son of the most evil syndicate of people to ever walk in Noelle, whose ancestors murdered thousands of my people, of Saeryn's people. His family has played a continuous part in the longest, most widespread, most malicious, most damning lie of all time. People in his family use to hunt dragonborn and rape them, rob them, skin them alive, eviscerate them, carry out all other kinds of atrocities against them. For centuries. Relentlessly for years and years and years. It's because of people like him that my mother is dead, my father, Marvo, my friends, *your* friends. How many millions of corpses can point to his family as the cause of their death? So I'm happy to see you, but there is nothing about your feelings that is okay."

"Andie... I love him."

"Then love someone else!"

The two girls stood face to face, not furious, but firm, immovable. Saeryn stood nearby, unsure of what to do or if she should do anything at all. Andie slowly shook her head, trying to deny that this was happening or that she'd heard these words, still unbelieving. Yara stood with her arms held to her sides, overjoyed to be reunited with her friend and exonerated, but unwilling to abandon what she has gained in the meantime.

Eventually, Andie reached for her bag and turned for the door.

"Saeryn's right," she said. "We need to get out of the city and regroup with the warriors outside."

She left without waiting for the others to get their things. Fortunately, it didn't take Saeryn and Yara long to catch up. The three women took the elevator down to the main floor and Andie poked out into the hall cautiously. She looked both ways and then checked for cameras, wishing they had been able to save the craiceanns. She saw one of the city police approaching and quickly leaned back inside the elevator, readying her hand to cast at him as soon as he was close enough.

"Andie, it's fine," Yara said. "You don't need to fight him."

"Me versus an overweight street cop? Not much of a fight."

"No, I mean I've taken care of it. No policeman in the city of New Carthage is going to give us any trouble."

Andie turned to face Yara, incredulous.

"And exactly how did you manage to do that?"

"When I first arrived in the city, I put on the craiceann I was wearing when you and I crossed paths, but while you were unconscious I just figured it would be easier if we didn't have to worry about sneaking around. I told you. Any police force can be bought for the right price."

"Well then."

Andie exited the elevator briskly and headed straight for the front of the hotel. As she passed the officer, he looked at her just long enough to register her face and then he turned deliberately away. So did the two guards standing at the entrance doors. Even the concierge conspicuously tucked his head into a book. They made it outside and just as they reached the street, a police car pulled up and stopped in front of them.

"I'm here to escort you to the outskirts of the city."

"What?" Andie asked, confused, looking behind and beside her to make sure the man was talking to her.

"You're the three, right? Andie, Saeryn, and Yara?"

"Yeah..."

"I'm your escort."

Andie looked over to Yara, who nodded in return. Saeryn needed no convincing and got in without hesitation, as if it were the most normal thing in the world. Andie was still looking at Yara.

"I can't believe you bought off the police. How much money do you have, anyway?"

"The real kicker is that I paid them in money I got from fencing the godhearts I stole from them."

The drive to the city wall was relatively long; the hotel was considerably further from the last place Andie was before she fainted. As the buildings passed her window, Andie reflected on how wonderful the city would be to visit under better circumstances, even if a large number of buildings were unfinished. As they rolled along, Andie counted at least seven major construction sites, and they went through several detours. Andie didn't say anything the entire car ride, though Saeryn and Yara spoke in low tones beside her. Soon enough the car was dropping the three of them off outside of the gates. Saeryn led them over into the woods where the dragonborn were waiting anxiously. Saeryn's dragon came over to her and nuzzled her with its massive, enchanting face. Once the dragonborn warriors saw Yara, they looked shocked, and not a bit defensive.

"Apologies for the delay," said Saeryn. "But as you can see, we ran into a ghost. We'd best be going now."

The warriors mounted up and so did Saeryn.

"I'll see you all soon," Yara said, taking a few steps back.

"What do you mean?" Andie asked. "You're coming with us."

"I can't. I can't ride your dragons."

"But they can still carry you in their arms. It won't be the most comfortable, but—"

"I have another mission, Andie. And Bonhaus is waiting for me."

"Right."

The two girls watched each other, maybe waiting to see what the other would do. Andie was so furious and so confused that a part of her just wished the moment were over. But another part of her thought about Yara and how intelligent, brave, and strong she had to be to do everything she did on her own. She wanted to say something, anything, to let Yara know that she appreciated her. That she missed her.

"Did you tell the police who we are?" she asked. "If they know that we're not only dragonborn, but the Queen and princess, it'll be a diplomatic nightmare. They haven't chosen a side yet and there's still hope they could side with us."

"No, they don't know. I told them our first names, but they're not bright enough to figure it out. I don't know if anyone in this city has ever even seen a dragonborn before. As for them choosing sides, I don't know if they'll formally align with you, but I told them it was the battalion who stole from the godhearts, so I know they won't be siding with them. Speaking of, here."

Yara reached in her backpack and pulled out a

smaller satchel. She opened it and Andie saw that it was full of godhearts. Gorgeous, priceless godhearts.

"I may have left out the part about my own pillaging. Take these with you. You'd be amazed how many doors open up to you when you tell people you have some."

"Thank you. When will we see you again?"

"Saeryn tells me you know how to operate the portals now. I'll go back to Bonhaus' mansion and wait there. When you get back to Arvall and you're ready for me just come through the portal. I'll be there."

"You and him."

"Me and Bonhaus."

Andie slide the satchel over her head and onto her shoulder. She turned from Yara.

"Take care of yourself," she said.

"You, too, Andie."

Andie got up on the dragon behind Saeryn and the party lifted off. Yara turned and headed on to her work.

CHAPTER FIFTEEN

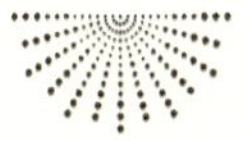

THREE DAYS LATER, ANDIE AND SAERYN STOOD AT the entrance to the Black Grotto, on the southern coast of Noelle. It was the most sinister looking place Andie had ever seen. Every inch of the environment was blacker than any night sky she'd ever laid eyes on: the stone, the grass, even the water flowing through the grotto and the walls of the grotto itself. The air was thick and moved in acidic layers, the result of some dark incantation. They had not seen or heard a single life form within a hundred kilometers of the place and even the dragons, bravest of beasts, were unsteady here.

A day and a half before, Andie and the party landed just behind the suburban outskirts of Mastield, a wealthy southern city and the home of House Urania. The journal said the portal was hidden somewhere on the family's property, House Urania being rather paranoid and extremely suspicious. When they couldn't figure out how to proceed after an entire afternoon and morning of thought, Andie took a page from Yara's book and broke into the estate, finding the head of the family enjoying a brandy in the cigar room. He was the oldest son of Rasputraenir, whom the Chancellor had killed at the University. After a painful episode, he'd told Andie of a legend he remembered. The story ended with the family's most prized possession being stolen by an unknown group of infiltrators and taken away to the south. Andie and Saeryn searched the papers in the family's vault and discovered a watchlist of the family's enemies. Andie had heard of most of the groups and knew most of them didn't have the resources or foresight to know House Urania had a portal, let alone break in and take it. Saeryn was able to exclude a few more. Eventually, they were left with a list of five.

They spent the next day moving through Mastield and interrogating the groups on their list. Two of the groups had lost all their power and disbanded years ago. One had been completely forgotten when all of its members were slaughtered in a retaliation attack by a rival group. Another group was still together and still neck deep in dastardly deeds, but had absolutely nothing useful to say, even when Andie started breaking their bones. The final group on their list had split into organizations, one involved in corporate espionage and the other in the sale of black market goods. The latter sounded most promising, but Saeryn went to speak to the corporate group anyway. By the time they gathered that morning, Andie had gotten the location of the "large, round thing" the black-market group had stolen and Saeryn had turned the police onto the corporate espionage group.

Now they were there, at the Black Grotto, hesitant to go in, when they finally decided to enter, Saeryn instructed the warriors to follow them at a distance of one hundred meters. Just as a precaution.

"I've seen some shady places in my day," said Andie. "But this is the worst. By far."

"I can taste the dark magic in the very air," Saeryn said. "I fear terrible things characterize the history of this place."

"I'm more worried about terrible things happening today. It's getting harder to see."

The deeper they went into the grotto, the less they could discern about their environment. Eventually, the light was no more than a dot far behind them.

"*Solas*," Andie and Saeryn say in unison.

Light appeared as a ball in each of their hands, but it didn't shine very far. The magic of the grotto was strong. The dragonborn warriors behind them echoed the spell and still there was hardly any light at all. In fact, as each new light came into the dark, the power of the other lights dimmed considerably and by the time the final warrior cast her spell, the lights of all were almost completely extinguished. Andie noticed this.

"Wait," she said. "Myra, put your light out again."

The warrior extinguished her light and the rest grow brighter.

"Now you, Thydron."

The next warrior extinguished his light and again the rest grow brighter.

"Every further light brought to the darkness decreases the ones already lit," Saeryn said. "What manner of magic lies in these walls?"

"I don't know, but I'm liking it less by the second," Andie said, looking around her. "Okay, everyone put out your light. Saeryn will hold hers and we'll all have to stick close."

Andie put out her light and so did the rest. Saeryn's light grew much brighter, but it still showed no more than a couple meters ahead. Andie moved closer to Saeryn and put her hand on the Queen's shoulder. They move forward.

Deeper and deeper they went, surprised and dismayed by how deep the grotto ran. The only sound was that of the black water flowing back the way they came. Aside from that, it was eerily quiet. The black of the grotto was so pure and impenetrable that Andie began to believe she could taste it, feel the darkness coming over her skin. She's not afraid, but she grows more and more suspicious that they're following bad information. She can't see above them, but she can tell from the way the sound changed that the ceiling has opened, grown more cavernous.

"Saeryn, throw your light up," she said. "I want to see what we've gotten ourselves into."

Saeryn took the light and formed a hard ball. She threw it up and it just kept going higher until they lost sight of it. They waited. A few moments passed and then the tiny ball came into view again as it fell. Andie was not at all pleased with their circumstances; it reminded her too much of the months they spent hiding in the tunnels beneath the University. As the light came back down to find Saeryn's hand they all jumped back in terrible surprise and then the light went out. Just before the light was gone they got a glimpse of a man's torso, heavily muscled and shirtless, tall and fierce and standing not one meter from Saeryn's face.

"The Dead are here," is all Saeryn managed to say.

"We've been here for days," said the man in front of them, his voice moving through the darkness like floating death. "Waiting for you or the other one, the one who has already taken two of our portals. Perhaps you thought we would not find you or that we would not realize what you and your friends are plotting. But don't worry, our men will have caught up with her and her lover by now."

His voice made Andie's skin crawl. It was made all the more terrifying because the light had gone out and they were in absolute darkness. She began to hear movement on every side. It is the Dead, moving in the shadows, along the walls, even in the water. She realized she didn't hear them before because they didn't want her to.

"Perhaps you aren't familiar with the abilities of the Dead," said a different voice. "Our senses give us the advantage. I can see, smell, and hear you in here as well as if it were daylight. I can taste your sweat on the air. You're afraid. The darkness troubles you. Your training and your nerves are failing."

"You reek of despair," said yet another voice. "You cannot fathom the fate that awaits you. You come for a treasure you cannot contain and you seek safety beyond this war. But hope is not a thing you should aspire to. Embrace your death. Cede all control."

"Sorry to disappoint," Andie said. "But we're not really in a dying kind of mood."

With a single deft movement she exploded fire out from her body; the purple flames erupted in all directions eluminating the grotto with blinding flashes of colorful light.

"Child," said a voice in the dark. "The Dead do

not feel flames. You forget, that we, too, descend from the dragon."

"Oh, I wasn't trying to hurt you. I only wanted to see how many of you there are."

And she had. Andie knew that there were seven Dead in the grotto. Two in front. Three behind. One clinging to the wall beside her. One in the water. She tapped Saeryn their number and locations on her arm.

"Now!" Saeryn called.

In an instant, the grotto was alive with magic and power. Every other spell the dragonborn cast was fire, not to hurt but to illuminate. But the fight was quickly going against them; the Dead are quick, strong, and the darkness is nothing to them. Try as they might, the dragonborn were barely able to stay on their feet. Andie was no sooner up than she was knocked down again. She couldn't see anything at all and all she heard was the sound of the Dead flashing by and the dragonborn being beaten mercilessly. They would all be dead already if it weren't for the dragonborn healing. Then one of the Dead lifted her in their arms, holding her so tight she could feel her bones about to break.

"Fhealltóir Fola," the Dead said.

Andie struggled to work her hands up, to raise them across each other and place them on the forearms of the Dead. When she finally touched him, she cast a desiccation spell. The man cried out in pain and then his voice faded into a terrible croak before she heard a dull thud in the dark.

"One down!" she called.

She barely had the words out of her mouth before another Dead hit her. She felt herself flying up into the air and colliding with the wall. She dropped what must have been ten meters to collide back with the ground. She laid there for a moment, recovering.

"One down!" Saeryn called.

At the sound of the good news, Andie began to pick herself up. No sooner was she on her feet than the hand of a Dead wrapped around her throat from behind.

"Goodbye traitor," the woman whispered.

"Not today," Andie said. "*Spiorad.*"

Andie's body became incorporeal and she stepped backward, moving right through the Dead. The woman was totally baffled and by the time she turned around to look behind her, Andie was already blasting a bolt of lightning through her chest. The terrific light of the bolt illuminated the cave and Andie watched as the woman was blown far over to the other side of the grotto and collided with the wall, causing a small avalanche of stones to fall on her.

"One down!" Andie called.

There was a great sucking of air and stone for a moment and then it disappeared. Andie recognized the magic: a vortex spell she and Saeryn taught their people after finding it in an old grimoire.

"One do—"

The voice of the dragonborn warrior was cut short by a bloodcurdling slicing sound. Andie heard the body of the warrior thud against the grotto floor.

"One down!" Saeryn called.

Andie put her back against the wall, preparing herself for the next assault. Soon enough, she heard the sound of a Dead flashing by and felt a cold pain cut upward across her torso. She screamed and folded her arm over the wound, feeling the blood come thick and fast. What terrified her the most was that she wasn't healing. At all. The wound hurt so badly she had to scream again. The Dead flashed by once more and sliced Andie's face. Then again to cut the back of her hand. Bleeding, in pain, and furious Andie forced herself to her feet and raised her good hand.

"*Eitilt mall comhlacht.*"

As Andie uttered the time curse the whole grotto froze. She began to feel her way forward. The first body was Saeryn; Andie could feel some blood on her, but she seemed fine. She moved over some more and nearly tripped over someone's corpse. She continued to feel around until her hand landed on the torso of a shirtless and heavily muscled warrior. She drew her sword and plunged it through the center of his chest. Moving on, she came across a dragonborn warrior in mid fall, badly injured, but possibly able to survive. It took her a few moments to locate the last Dead, who was in midair, frozen as she leapt to grab hold of the wall. Andie pushed her sword forward and felt it drive home with a grave slide.

"*Eitilt ar ais.*"

Time returned to normal. The Dead have been defeated, but Andie wondered at what cost.

"Any dragonborn still alive, identify yourself!" she called.

"I'm here," Saeryn said. "Multiple wounds, but nothing life-threatening."

"I'm here, too," Andie said. "I have a pretty bad cut on my chest, but I should be fine. Is there anyone else?"

There was only silence. Andie waited. Silence.

"Anyone? Please!"

"Still... here."

The voice sounded as if it was drowning in its own blood. Andie turned to it and felt her way toward the voice. She heard Saeryn moving as well. She reached the fallen warrior and knelt in the dark.

"Myra, is that you?"

"Vernaylia... Vernaylia..."

"You're going to be fine," Saeryn said, reaching them. "As soon as we get you outside we'll take a look at you. Just hold on."

"I'm not... healing... my Queen... what did they... do to me?"

"They have evolved."

Andie stood, unsteadily, and tried to orient herself in the dark. She casts a ball of light.

"I'm going to look for the portal," she said. "Try to keep her conscious."

"No, Andie. We need to get Vernaylia help now. Help me lift her, as quick as you can."

"We came all this way, I'm not turning back now. We just lost our entire group."

"One is still alive and we might save her if we go now. You promised me, Andie! You promised to put your people first."

"That's what I'm doing."

Andie held the light out in front of her and hurried off deeper into the dark. She knew there was no time to waste and ran as fast as she could without running into the wall, all along clutching the horrible wound on her chest. Before long she heard the sound change again and knew the space was getting smaller, that she was reaching the end. She heard water ahead and slowed. As she drew near the sound, the light shone on a broken thing, round, ornate, and protruding out of the water. She leaned forward to see it better.

"No."

It was a piece of the portal and as she walked along

the water's edge, she saw more pieces. It had been destroyed. She took a minute to register the result, the disappointment, then raced back to find Saeryn and Vernaylia. She and Saeryn helped the wounded warrior walk the long path back to the light and when they finally exited the Black Grotto, Andie had never been so happy to see sun. All three collapsed into the black grass. Andie looked over at Vernaylia and saw that she was bruised and cut on nearly every inch of her body. It wasn't until Andie saw that her eyes were glazed, her body still, that she realized the girl was dead. She probably died while they were carrying her.

Andie looked past Vernaylia to Saeryn, who had a deep cut on her back and appeared to have been pierced just inside of her shoulder. She also had a cut down her neck which only nearly missed her jugular artery. Andie looked down to assess her own wounds. She couldn't see the bruises, but she could feel them healing. She probably sustained at least one broken rib on each side, but those were healing, too. The cuts, however, were serious. The one on her face was not so bad and had already stopped bleeding, but she needed to bandage the one on the back of her hand quickly because it showed no signs of stopping. The cut on her chest was just beginning to clot, with the help of her clothes and armor, but it was deep and long. It would need stitches.

"Was it there?" Saeryn asked. "Did you find the portal?"

"It was there, but it's destroyed."

"Was it at the very back of the grotto?"

"Yes."

"And was there water there, a pond?"

"Yes. How did you know?"

"Legend tells of a cruel sorcerer who once lived in this place, performing all manner of evil and forbidden magic. They say the only person who could get close enough to kill him was his wife, who had lived as his slave and victim for years. As he was leaning over the pond to drink, his wife crept up behind him and slit his throat. She spilled all of his blood into the pond, but it was poisoned blood, full of magic so hateful it cannot even be uttered. The horrid power of his blood cursed this place, turned the air and the water sour. If the stories are to be believed, the pond at the back of the grotto can destroy anything that touches its surface."

"That portal is gone forever," Andie said, rolling on her back to rest. "Shame. I really wanted it. But this is better than it being used against us."

"Fine. Now let's tend to Vernaylia."

Saeryn rolled onto her side and crawled to Vernaylia. She tried to shake her awake.

"Vernaylia. Vernaylia."

When she realized the girl was dead, she went silent. Still. Nothing moved but her tears.

———

THE PORTAL STIRRED in the Archives at the bottom of Leabharlann. Two battalion soldiers emerged. They synchronized their watches and started their countdown. They rushed up from the Archives and through Leabharlann. They entered the hall and went separate directions. One of them went out through the front of the University, snapping the neck of the first person he ran into and hiding the body. He hurried along the front of the black marble, surveying the area and noting the position of the few guards. He saw that scores of people were getting off SKY 6 and passing through a checkpoint to go into the University. He turned on his camouflage and took up a position where he could observe.

The other soldier was still inside and had turned on his camouflage, too. He moved through the University, staying close to the walls to avoid detection. He reached the main hub and saw that it was filled with the citizens of Arvall who had fled to the University for protection. They were moving down into the tunnels and corridors, the bowels and deep caves of both modern usage and the ancient coin mint. Most of the city was here, with the exception of those who opted for the shelters in the city. He stayed long enough to gather some small intelligence. He checked his watch and headed back toward Leabharlann.

The soldiers reached the library at the same time. They hurried through the library, back into the Archives. But when they returned, the room was full of people. They were coming up from the portal at the dock in Arvall. The soldiers went unnoticed and stuck near the edge of the room. When that batch of citizens ended, the soldiers hurried to the portal and whispered the words they had been taught. The portal changed shades. The soldiers jumped in.

They came out in front of the army, high on the silver cliff that lines Gordric's Pain. The two soldiers walked over to the group of Beautiful Dead who had been placed in charge of the army

"I saw people getting off the train and going in," the first soldier said. "I overheard that Arvall City is completely empty. The train and the portal have been running nonstop. Everyone in the city is either in shelters under Arvall or in the University."

"They're vulnerable," said the second soldier. "They've tried to set up what security they can, but they don't have the numbers to protect an entire city. They can't even match our army. I heard their professors saying they only have a standing force of less than six thousand. They've been expecting more aid to come, but so far they haven't received any. They've heard about what Beladorion and the rest of the Dead did to the dragonborn in the Hot Salts and it has them all panicked. They're terrified. Most of their army is students and professors, and most of them come from privilege and peace. They'll never be able to stand against us. People were coming into the University through a portal and I would guess the other end is somewhere near the bottom of the mountain, in the city. Once we infiltrate the University, it will only take a handful of men to cover the entrances to the tunnels and corridors and hold them hostage in their own refuge."

"Such excellent news," the Dead general said. "I'm almost saddened to think the battle will be so easily won, though I trust there will be quite a satisfying amount of bloodshed before the door is shut on this war. What of the leaders?"

"Lymir, the head of the University, has apparently fallen into depression. They haven't been able to get him to say much the last few days. Raesh, the son of the council fighters' deceased leader, is running their defenses now. Capable enough and worth watching. Oren, their greatest dragonborn warrior and general, was killed in the Hot Salts. There are some other fighters of considerable strength who have a hand in the strategy as well. And I heard they have a professor, a Marcus, who knows how to operate the portals, which could work against us."

"I see. And what of the Queen of the blood traitors? What of their princess?"

"They're not there."

All the heads in the proximity turned to the soldier.

"What do you mean?" the Dead general asked.

"I mean they're not in the University or the city. They left days ago on a mission to cure the Maeludrax we spread in the True Isles. No one has heard from them since."

"Strange. The dragonborn do not contract disease, so they cannot have become sick. Assuming they've rediscovered the healing properties of their blood, they will have long since cured the Thabians and restarted the supply line. That would have taken mere hours. With an army marching on their city they wouldn't waste time there when their mission was complete, so where did they go? Of course. You mentioned a portal at the foot of the mountain. Before they only had one now they have two. It would appear they've gotten their hands on some very old and critical information. They found the portal in Thabes and had it shipped back to Arvall to help with the evacuation efforts. If they knew about one, then they would've known about the others as well, which means they went to find them. From the True Isles the closest destination is New Carthage, yet I know for a fact that Beladorion already has that portal and the one in Raven Deep. The portals of House Clio and House Polyhymnia are too far out of their reach and even if they risk some adventure, they wouldn't be willing to travel so far. That means that just now they're either at or near the Black Grotto and they won't be coming back from there. Beladorion will have figured out what they're up to and sent Dead to meet them. Strange news, but fortunate. We will attack now."

The general turned to give the order. The order was repeated all the way through the ranks, the columns, until it was spread through the entire army. They began to move forward. The battalion soldiers and the Beautiful Dead stood aside to let the rest go through first. Line after line of soldiers passed into the portal.

"We'll send two thousand men into the University," the general said. "Six thousand into the city. Two thousand will continue on foot and bring the portal. Three waves, three locations, one unstoppable assault."

CHAPTER SIXTEEN

In the University, Raesh and Sarinda oversaw the sheltering of the citizens of Arvall. Reports came up from the foot of the mountain confirming that they had finally succeeded in evacuating the city. They smiled, happy to finally have that much off their minds. They walked to the center of the main hub, through which the final citizens were moving on their way to the tunnels.

"Who knew watching people walk could be so exhausting?" Sarinda asked, reclining.

"Well, when they number in the millions..."

"Right. How deep do these tunnels and corridors go anyway?"

"Deep. I don't think anyone's actually been all the way to the end in this cycle. I'm just going to lie here for a minute, rest, and then get back to the hospital."

"I'm coming with you. I can't believe Carmen's awake. How is she?"

"She's strong. Really strong," Raesh said, sitting up a little. "They still aren't sure what kind of magic caused it or what exactly it did to her. Whatever they were giving her in that drip before was helping to keep her under and they didn't know it. As soon as the doctor changed her medicine, she woke up. I'm so happy I can hardly think. She's already trying to walk."

"Andie's going to be so happy when she gets back. I know she's really missed her, we all have."

Just then they were startled by the sound of screaming. They leapt up and ran in the direction of the noise, but they were met by a phalanx of soldiers. Their instincts saved them. Raesh and Sarinda were casting before they even fully understood what was happening. The soldiers were strong and had been well trained by the Beautiful Dead, but they weren't trained for the hallways Sarinda and Raesh knew so well. The two fought back against the soldiers furiously and soon more professors came to their aid. What the professors lacked in fighting ability, they made up for in sheer knowledge. Raesh and his fellows fought admirably, but more and more soldiers were pouring from Leabharlann and marching down every hallway. Raesh knew it was only a matter of moments before they were surrounded.

"We've got to get back to the tunnels!" he called. "We can regroup and plan a defense, but we've got to move, now!"

They began to retreat, casting behind them and running as fast as they could amidst flying spells and flying debris from hexes exploding into the walls. As they reached the main hub, the citizens who had yet to enter the tunnels saw the coming army and began to panic. They flew to wherever they thought they were safest, leaving all their things behind. A few brave souls turned and tried to fight, but they were cut down instantly by the well-trained battalion. Raesh, Sarinda, and the professors held the battalion off just long enough to get the final stragglers into the tunnel, then they all entered. Once they crossed the barrier, Raesh touched the tunnel wall, which initiated the magic seal to keep the enemy out.

"I don't understand," Sarinda said, still gasping. "How did they get inside? How did they even get within ten kilometers of the city without us knowing?"

"I don't know," Raesh said, slumping to the floor. "This isn't right. They weren't supposed to be here for another week. We were supposed to have more time."

"Well, however they did it they're here now. What about this seal? Will it hold?"

"Yeah. We've been working on them for months, before we even knew an army was coming. Nobody gets through that we don't want to get through."

"Andie and Saeryn, wherever you two are, we need you now," Sarinda said, closing her eyes and trying to catch her breath. "There's no way we're going to win this without you."

Outside the seal, the soldiers set up a dense patrol to guard the tunnel entrances and commence trying to break in. The entrance to each tunnel was guarded by fifty soldiers, each armed to the teeth and dead-set on ending life in Arvall. The tunnels were full of screams, cries, and prayers. The people had been told about the terror and senselessness of war, but few of them had ever truly seen it. All of them were waiting for her to return, for Andie to cut the sky on the back of a dragon and save them.

Column after column of soldiers filed in through the Archives, up and out through Leabharlann, and then into the University. They went down every hall, tunnel, corridor, and passageway that hadn't been sealed off. They checked every room, lecture hall, closet, laboratory, and office. They found no innocents to terrorize, but they destroyed everything they touched, leaving trails of fire and debris all throughout the newly renovated university. They blew up whole sections of rooms, disintegrated critical loadbearing pillars. They filed out to the mountainside and begin ensuring that none would escape, blocking anything that even remotely resembled an entrance or exit. They stationed themselves across the mountainside and took up positions.

In Arvall City below, the next wave of the army swept into the city streets from the portal there. Professor Iceubes was still at the portal, attempting to perform a few final calibrations, when the second wave started. The soldier who killed him did not even give him a chance for his life, but merely ran him through with a spear of black bronze. The soldiers set about discovering the hidden shelters in the city. With the training they had received from the Dead, it wasn't as difficult as it should have been. However, the citizens were not completely helpless; knowing they would be ill equipped to physically take on the coming army, the citizens had set up traps over seventy-five percent of the city. Mines, darts, blades, tar, and other traps were soon going off as the army marched through the city. Even that was not enough because the army's sheer numbers guaranteed their progress. As some of the shelters were found, the soldiers commenced trying to break through the protective magic and barricades, hungry for death.

At last it was time for the battalion and the Dead to emerge from the portal. The battalion marched out in perfect ranks, strong, fierce, undeniable. Their sleek and powerful armor shone in the sun and their march shook the ground. They were bent on destruction. The Dead came through the portal too fast for the eye to track, racing through the city streets, effortlessly sensing and avoiding the traps. They leapt and climbed the buildings looking for vantage points and lives to end.

Raesh and Sarinda sat in the tunnel of the University, thinking how they might get out of this mess.

***

"This is no time for one of your lectures, Saeryn."

"Then perhaps you'd like to schedule a later time for me to remind you of what damage the time spell can do? Do you truly need reminding of what it has done to your people, to you yourself not so long ago?"

"I did what I had to do," Andie said, turning from Saeryn to continue tending the wound across her chest.

"No, you did what you wanted to do. And you used a spell that is not only heinous, but dark. Tampering with time is no meager thing, princess, and if you had made even the slightest miscalculation or mispronunciation—"

"If this, if that. With you it's always about what could go wrong. You never miss an opportunity to second guess me. Can't you ever just be happy I've saved your life?"

"Being prudent does not preclude my ability to be

grateful," Saeryn said, offended. "You act as if my berating you is a task I enjoy. You are not like other people, Andie. You're nothing like them at all. You cannot imagine the power in your blood. I know because it is the same blood that runs in my veins."

"Enough. I get it already. I'm special, I'm going to be Queen. You want me to put our people first, fine, but I'm going to do it my way. And I'll be glad when I'm Queen so I won't have to listen to these condescending tones anymore."

"You do not even see how far from the path you've strayed. Torturing people for information, putting your personal quests before your people, wasting precious time on missions you conjure up to soothe your own feeling of inadequacy, judging your friends—"

"What friends? Yara? She's in love with the enemy!"

"Do not tell me who the enemy is. I resisted and fought them as a child, and my friends and family were being slaughtered long before yours were ever born. Yara has traveled and worked on her own for months, winning priceless victories for our cause when we almost had her executed. I hardly think loving whom she loves should bar her from us. Unlike you, I trust her judgement."

"Why don't you just tell me what you're really upset about, Saeryn?"

"To put it bluntly, I worry that not only are you far from the girl I thought you were, but that you may never be fit to call yourself Queen."

Andie looked Saeryn squarely in the face, furious and hurt. She felt as if Saeryn had not only taken her birthright, but also threatened to cut her out from the dragonborn altogether, take away the last vestige of family she has.

"You would cut me out?" Andie asked, tears welling in her eyes.

"If I thought it was best for our people. I have told you time and time again that being a Queen is not easy, that it requires decisions that shake the very foundation of who you are. I love you, Andie. You have been a daughter and a friend and a partner to me. I would not cut you out willingly, but I cannot allow someone so caught up in their own pain to lead our people. And before you try to defend yourself, I must tell you what I know. I know you sneak down to the prisons and fight the Searchers and soldiers who have been imprisoned there. I know you've taken some of the grimoires from the collection. I know you've been studying dark magic. And I know that you found the Searcher who took your mother and I know what you've done to him. None of this makes you in any way fit to lead us or even join us. And if you think it brings me any pleasure to say this then you never knew me at all."

With that Saeryn turned from Andie and returned to tending her own wound. Andie turned, too, and lowered her head. She had no idea Saeryn had been watching her so closely. Now that she did know it dawned on her that Saeryn had spent every day hoping for her to change. Andie hadn't even realized how serious things had gotten. It started off so innocently. She fought in the prisons to train, test, strengthen herself. She took the grimoires, not to steal them, but to study the subjects she knew Saeryn wouldn't approve of and she only studied them because she knew they needed all the help they could get. But Saeryn was right. Andie had gone too far. She thought on this. And thought. And then she came to her decision, knowing it will shape the rest of her life.

"I don't care."

"What?" Saeryn asked, turning.

"I don't care. I don't care what you think of me or that you don't want me to be your Queen. I don't care that I'm reckless and selfish and that I'm willing to do anything to save the people you can't seem to protect yourself. I am bad. And angry. And hurting. And all those things have worked in me to get us here, alive. I pulled you from that portal. I tipped the scales in the Archives. I defeated the Chancellor and his battalion. I defeated Ashur. I saved those warriors from the Church. I found the portal in Thabes. I saved our lives in that grotto. What have you done? Walked around in all your dignity and integrity, judging me for getting my hands dirty when you knew you were too much of a coward to do those things yourself!"

"You forget your place, Andie," Saeryn said, rising. "I am your Queen and you will address me as such."

"As of right now, you're nothing but a means to an end. It's time to go. And when this is all over and I've saved the dragonborn and Arvall, then you can judge me while you sit back and enjoy the safe world I've handed to you."

Minutes later, they were in the air again, the other four dragons flying without riders behind them. By the next morning they should be back in Arvall. The search for the portals was at an end for the time being, the final portal the one belonging to House Melpomene, the Chancellor's family. Marcus' notes in the journal indicated that he believed the Chancellor had no idea that his family was in possession of a portal, but that he may have inadvertently had it sent to the Old World.

His research showed that the more power the Chancellor acquired, the more paranoid he grew. He was convinced the other families were plotting to steal his wealth; he arranged to have several barges of his most valuable assets sailed across the Spider Sea, including a wooden container described as being twenty-five meters long, thirteen wide, and ten deep, more than enough space to hold a portal among other family heirlooms. But those are thoughts for another day. Right then, Andie's mind was tuned to one thing and one thing only. Violence.

ON THE OUTSKIRTS OF ABHAINN, Lucas moved through the camp, ignoring both the dragonborn captives he passed and the crashing claps of thunder from the Hot Salts in the distance. They had finally moved out of that area the day before and had since already set up a portal that would take them straight to Arvall. Beladorion and the Dead appeared to know everything about the portals, every variation and fluctuation, yet Lucas had watched them very carefully as they manipulated it, just as he was directed to do. Now he made his way purposefully across the field to fulfill his mission. He entered the large black tent that sat at the head of the battalion forces.

Ashur was there, standing over a map that he read with great focus and intention. His burned and scarred face turned to look at Lucas when he entered. With a nod of his head, Lucas confirmed that his mission had been successful. Ashur nodded in return to express his gratitude. They began talking, making up a conversation that had nothing to do with what they wanted to talk about. They spoke of the weather, the war, the Hot Salts, any banal and common topic they could think of, because they knew that ears were listening.

By then they were fully aware of what the Dead were capable of and they knew that the only way to deceive them was to surprise them. An almost impossible task. Part of every battalion member's training was learning to communicate in two different sign languages, for instances when silence was critical. Lucas and Ashur sat down at the table and never stopped talking, yet they had a completely different conversation with their hands.

"I think I've figured out how we can get our autonomy back," Lucas signed.

"Good," signed Ashur. "When we first got into bed with these people I had no idea they would take us over so quickly, without our even noticing. But the victory must be ours. I don't plan on sharing anything."

"I apologize, my leader. You warned us this was a dangerous move, and though it may pay off in the end by helping us destroy the dragonborn, it may also destroy us. But I have found the secret of controlling the portal."

"Excellent work, Lucas. You can recalibrate it to find and connect to other portals?"

"Yes, my leader, to any of the portals that are

switched on."

"I'm not so sure they didn't let you learn how to control the portal as part of some master plan. We need to be careful now, more careful than we've ever been."

"I understand."

They laughed then, still having a completely different conversation by mouth than the very grave one they were having by hand. Lucas banged the table as if was the funniest thing he'd ever heard and Ashur gave a hearty laugh. Their hands told a different story.

"We need to kill these people," Ashur signed.

"Forgive me, leader, but we may not be able to."

"Have more faith in me, Lucas. I've had our engineers working on modifications for our suits since before we ever went groveling to the Dead. They tell me they're close to a solution. I believe that by the time we step through that portal it will be the Dead who are afraid."

"Excellent, my leader. Do you mean the engineers from Hessian's Bridge?"

"Yes. Our new recruits are proving indispensable. All we need to worry about now is making sure the Dead step through that portal as planned. As soon as they're all through we'll upgrade our suits and recalibrate the portal. By the time they figure out that we're no longer with them, we'll already be plunging our hands into their chests."

"I look forward to it. But—and forgive me if a I cross a line, my leader—but what about our forces who are already marching on Arvall. They won't know whose side to choose."

"They will either learn or die. We have no room for mercy now."

The night passed and the morning came. Lucas and Ashur did not so much as nod to each other when they came together with Beladorion. Ashur had guessed that Beladorion's bloodlust would outweigh his incredible intelligence, causing him to want to go through the portal first with his people. No sooner had the whole force gathered than the Dead began to go through the portal, dragging along the chained and captive dragonborn behind them. When all the captives have been taken through, the Dead flew the dragons through the portal. It seemed a kind of betrayal, that the dragons would allow the Dead to ride them, but no one quite understood how magic worked in the blood or how it passed things on from one species to the next hybrids. The dragons, after all, were only creatures. After some time, the Dead were finally all through, except Beladorion.

"We're not cannibals," he said, standing before the portal. "It's a common misconception. We don't like raw flesh and we don't eat human flesh at all. We don't care much for the taste of blood, though, to be fair, we don't mind it as much as others do. We will only have the blood of the traitors and only because it is the way to obtain their magic."

"And so you will," Ashur said. "When the time is right."

"The time is right when I say it is right," Beladorion said, rounding on Ashur. "I know you and your battalion are planning to cross us. I know that as soon as I step through this portal you'll have Lucas recalibrate so that you come out where you wish. Perhaps you thought you were actually fooling us. Perhaps you also thought we didn't know you were trying to enhance your suits."

"How could you know that?" asked Ashur.

"Because it's my business to know these things. Honestly, I haven't seen or heard anything to give you away, it was simply the logical thing to do. Think about it: you want the dragonborn destroyed, but you want to do it yourself because who would want to go through everything you've been through and not get the glory? Of course, you're going to try to go behind our backs because we're better than you and you can't confront us face to face, so you scheme and plot in the shadows. Not only that but we've practically taken all control from you and you want it back. And we've noticed your clumsy, dull-witted friend there lurking around. Your best and most logical course of action would be to let us go through the portal first, change it afterwards, come out in a different part of the city with enhanced suits and stab us through our backs when the fighting reaches its most intense. A perfectly reasonable plan except it's too reasonable, it's exactly what one should do in this situation. You lack creativity."

"But how did you know?"

"You're not very hard to figure out, commander. I wanted to know what you would do so I reasoned it out and now you've confirmed it. I would advise against this little coup of yours. We're willing to forgive you just this once. But I would advise this: if you do choose to cross us, don't miss."

Beladorion turned and stepped through the portal. Ashur stood still for a moment, looking into the portal and contemplating his next decision. Lucas and the entire battalion waited, anxious now that they know the Dead were onto them, but still undyingly loyal to their leader, Ashur. Finally, Ashur turned to Lucas.

"No one intimidates us. No one overshadows us. This is what we've trained for. A world with no more dragons or the abominations that came from them, and that includes the Dead. Let's end the war we started. Do it."

A cheer went through the battalion as Lucas set about his work of changing the destination. Ashur turned to his forces.

"Engineers! Engineers to my location, now!"

CHAPTER SEVENTEEN

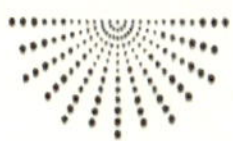

ANDIE AND SAERYN COULDN'T BELIEVE THEIR EYES. As they flew over the String Fields and Arvall came up across the horizon, they saw that the city was burning. The closer they went, the more damage they could see. Andie was shocked beyond words, having not expected the army to arrive for at least another week. She realized they were likely using the portals they had stolen to cover the distance. Tears came into her eyes as they flew lower and faster, desperate to reach the city to help.

As they finally breached the airspace over the city, Andie looked down into the streets and couldn't believe what she saw. No one was there. No one was mounting a defense or fighting back, aside from a few small skirmishes. She wondered where the professors and students were. Where Raesh was. She began to wonder if she had been gone too long, if she had lost everything and everyone because she gambled and lost. She didn't even know how long the army had been in the city.

Saeryn flew to where the army was thickest and then swooped the dragon straight down in a breathtaking nose dive, the other dragons following. The dragon slammed into the ground so hard the asphalt cracked. Saeryn and Andie dismounted and rushed to meet the army that was much too large for them to handle on their own. They were, above all, two of the bravest and most powerful women in Noelle, but still they were no match for what lay ahead.

Andie was the first into battle, casting furiously and swinging her blade with excruciating intensity. She cast an acid rain over a group of soldiers and parried the thrust of black and bronze spears. She opened the earth beneath them and then closed it over them. Her power had grown strong over the past year, and she held nothing back.

Saeryn came forward with as much grace as could be mustered when one was going into battle. She lifted a group of soldiers and then brought them crashing down onto the ground Andie had just sealed. She pulled glass from the windows of a nearby building and sent the glittering, razor-sharp cloud through the soldiers. The result was wave of crimson that painted the surrounding landscape in the colors of war. She drew her sword as well, though she swung it more cautiously than Andie.

They fought hard and long, staying at the edge of the army so that they wouldn't get surrounded or trapped. When they came across citizens in need, they helped as much as they could, half carrying them to safety, casting small healing spells in between offensive blasts of magic back toward the approaching enemies.

The army was well-trained in their short amount of time together, but they were still only a hodgepodge of men who had been soldiers for a few months. They could not match the power, skill, or intensity of the dragonborn women. Apart, Andie and Saeryn were a force to be reckoned with. Together, they were a formidable sight whose bravery would be carried down generation to generation through history books and bedtime stories. Both powerful dragonborn fueled each other's power, each drawing from the other and pushing everything they had into their magical attacks. Saeryn's magic was graceful, practiced. Andie's was more archaic, a ferocious mélange of sorcery and dragonborn magic.

The enemies fell one by one before Queen and princess. Andie was cautious of her surroundings, keeping a wary eye out for the Beautiful Dead, who she knew must already be there somewhere. They did come across some battalion soldiers, who posed a much graver threat than the simple soldiers. Andie took two down, as did Saeryn. They didn't go far before one of the soldiers regained his feet and, managing to surprise them, conjured a blade and sent it flying at Saeryn. The blade missed her organs, but cut a devastating gash in her side. Saeryn fell to her knees and Andie placed herself between the soldier and the Queen. She cast a spell that broke every bone in the soldier's body. She grabbed Saeryn and dragged her into a nearby building.

"You need to get over yourself," Andie said, kneeling to take Saeryn into her lap and held the wound until the dragon blood healed her. "This isn't a game."

"What are you talking about?"

"That soldier. If you had taken him out he never would have been able to do this to you."

"You mean if I'd killed him?"

"Yes, Saeryn. You need to kill. And I know you're not okay with that, but you need to get okay with it soon because if not, either you're going to die or you're going to get someone else killed."

"It may be easy for you, but I do not relish the thought of taking another's life."

"I don't like it either, Saeryn. It makes me sick inside. Sometimes I can't even sleep at night thinking about the things I've done, but I don't do them because they feel good. I don't do them because they're right. I do them because they're necessary. Thousands of trained and dangerous men have stormed our city and are roaming the streets killing innocent people. They can't be reasoned with or talked down. They've come thousands of miles to be here, to murder us. There's only one way this ends and that's with a pile of someone's bodies."

"But it never ends. The bloodshed never stops," Saeryn said, trying to control her emotion. "I have spent my entire life watching people die and it never gets easier. You think I don't realize the reality of war? That I don't understand our freedom isn't free? You forget I've killed before. So many I've killed. I thought that here, now, in a new time and a new place we could be different. I couldn't see how we could win this war if we fought the University with the very thing they used to destroy us—death."

"Saeryn the University didn't invent death, even if they perfected it. And everything they did was done in cruelty. I fight to survive, to protect our people and the people of Arvall who have risked their city and their lives so that we could have a home among them. Killing makes me sick, it makes me hate myself, it makes me hate war. I want what you want: peace, happiness, safety, a home. But all of that is in jeopardy now. We can't afford to spare the lives of thousands of evil soldiers. We don't have the prison space to hold them because the cells are already full of people we've spared. We have to let the world know that we won't continue to be bullied, to be ambushed. Do you understand?"

Saeryn was silent for a moment, healing there in Andie's arms. Andie held her close, wondering if the Queen of the dragonborn would do what was right or what was necessary. The two women had such differences and such love for one another.

"Perhaps I had forgotten," Saeryn said. "How it is to rule when the threat is imminent. My mother was the one who told me that being a Queen is about making difficult, but fair decisions. Later, when I led the rebellion, I learned that her wisdom was slightly incomplete. Being a Queen is about making difficult, but fair decisions and sometimes those decisions are about whether or not lives should be spared."

"And what will you do, Saeryn?"

"Protect my people."

"At all costs?"

"At all costs."

Fully healed from the wound, Saeryn began to raise herself. Andie helped her to her feet. They shared a look, but only for a moment. Then they return to the street. To the war.

One of the citizens they helped earlier had made his way back to his shelter. Once he had been seen to and treated, he moved through the crowded space to the back room, where all of the communications devices were. He was a radio operator, helping to relay information and keep the other shelters and the University tunnels informed of the progress. He had only stepped outside for a moment to get a better sense of what was happening. Now that he had returned, he re-took his seat and turned on his equipment. He took a deep breath and got to work.

"All stations, all stations, all stations. Critical update. Diamonds have been found in the streets, diamonds have been found in the streets. Two diamonds, two diamonds a little rough for wear, but still shining, still shining. Repeat: two diamonds have been found in the streets, still shining."

"…TWO DIAMONDS a little rough for wear, but still shining, still shining. Repeat: two diamonds have been found in the streets, still shining."

As the transmission came in over the radio, the professors and students who were familiar with the code began to rejoice. It was the only good news they'd had since the attack began the day before. They spread the word through the tunnels and corridors, and people began to cheer up for the first time since they left their homes.

When Raesh heared the news, his heart began to

race. he hadn't said anything to anybody, but he had begun to seriously worry something had happened to Andie. There weren't words to describe how happy he was to hear that she and Saeryn were safe, were back, and were fighting. He jumped up to his feet and listened to broadcast again, just to be sure he heard correctly. Sarinda was on her feet as well, almost as relived as Raesh was. They embraced, thrilled to finally have some news in their favor.

"We have to go help them," Sarinda said. "Somehow, someway, we've got to fight through this army and get down to the city. Once they figure out Andie and Saeryn are back this army is going to rush down to the city to overwhelm them."

"I know, but first I need to get to my apartment. There's something Andie's going to need and I can't go down without it."

"I'll go with you. But first we have to organize our forces here. You and I fought these guys, so I know you saw what I saw."

"Trained, but still not soldiers."

"Exactly. Raesh, there were a lot of these guys, but I think we just might be able to take them or at least make them think twice about this assault. Now's the time. Everyone's getting excited about the return of the Queen and princess. We shouldn't wait any longer."

"Agreed. You try to find Lymir and I'll get on the radio."

Sarinda took off down into the tunnel and Raesh hurried over to the small station they had set up near the mouth of the tunnel.

"All stations, all stations, all stations," he began. "This is Raesh. I know we're supposed to be using code, but the enemy is already here and they don't care what we're saying. They just want to kill us. I want all of you to know that Andie and Saeryn have returned, they're back. I know some of you felt that they'd abandoned us, but they're down on the streets of the city right now, fighting alone against an army of thousands. I know you all have families and lives that you want to get back to, but I'm asking every able-bodied person with enough training and courage to stand with us.

"In just a few moments I'm going to lead a charge out of the tunnel. I know these are dark times and I know we're in an impossible position, but believe me when I say this fight is far from over. What I'm asking for now might turn out to be the ultimate sacrifice and maybe I'll go down, too, but what I won't do is sit back and watch while a cruel army destroys my city, my friends, my family, and my entire way of life. By coming here and declaring war on us they've challenged everything we believe in. I'm not going to allow that.

"I have power in my body and a girl I love who's fighting for us right now. We may not love her in the same way or for the same reasons, but I know you love her, too. I'm going now to fight the fight of my life and if I die I'll do it honorably and with the knowledge that as long as my heart beat I fought them with everything I had. If this is the end, let it be one they will never forget."

Raesh signed off and suddenly the University was alive with applause. All through the tunnels, passages, and corridors the people clapped, excited and inspired. All around him people were getting to their feet and preparing to go out and fight. Raesh himself felt a little more emboldened now. Soon Sarinda returned.

"Raesh, you're not going to believe this."

Lymir came in a few paces behind her, dragging a man through the dirt.

"What's going on?" Raesh asked.

"This is Murphy," Lymir said, throwing the man down at Raesh's feet. "Murphy is a spy, a mole for the battalion."

"What? Are you sure?"

"Positive. I've been unsteady for about a week now, thinking that something wasn't right. It was that attack that Sarinda reported. I kept wondering how that advanced party could get all the way to the dock without being seen, and how they even knew to go there. I did some investigating and found some correspondence on the body of one of their soldiers. I knew then there was a mole. I had no idea who, though, so I had to be careful about what I said. That's why I've been so quiet when it came to discussing strategy. I managed to narrow down the suspect list by finding out who even had the clearance to know about Sarinda's mission. From there I knew it had to be someone in the communications department because they would have the ability and resources to contact the advanced party and track Sarinda's boat as soon as it was close enough to the city, because no one had heard from her in months. I was really struggling to narrow it down from there, but then I caught this little weasel trying to hijack a signal back there. and he told me where I can find the rest of Ash's spies. Investigation complete."

"It's great to have you back," Raesh said. "Don't dispose of him yet, though, he may prove useful. Sarinda and I are about to attack."

"Go," said Lymir, his foot on Murphy's neck. "I'll get on the radio and give the notice."

"What notice?"

"The notice for the secret groups of trained professors and council fighters I stashed around the city. You didn't think I was just sitting back enjoying the view the last week, did you?"

Raesh smiled and turned to Sarinda. She nodded to him and they both turned toward the tunnel.

Outside the shield, the soldiers saw that something was about to happen. They stood, squared off, prepared their weapons for use or their hands for casting. Raesh touched the wall and the shield came down. Sarinda wasted no time and released a wave of magic that took the thirty nearest soldiers off their feet. As Raesh's seal came down, so did the others. The people had finally been roused to action. Raesh and Sarinda led the charge. They were magnificently brutal, showing no mercy to the men who had shown no mercy to them. Professors and students from all the tunnels came rushing out, and in no time the soldiers in the main hub were overwhelmed and calling for reinforcements.

Raesh and Sarinda made their way to SKY 1 and boarded it. The train took off. It climbed steeply at first, before making its customary journey out to the mountainside for the spiral ascent. Just as Raesh allowed himself to relax, a spell nearly took his head off. He cast back in retaliation, hitting the soldier right in the chest and knocking him off his feet. They hadn't even thought to check to make sure the train was safe. A mistake they would be sure never to make again.

CHAPTER EIGHTEEN

Soldiers came pouring into the train car at both ends. Raesh and Sarinda fought back to back fending off spells, spears, and bullets. The train sustained serious damage, but continued its ascent. Raesh and Sarinda fought the soldiers all the way to the summit. The train stopped and the fight spilled out onto the platform.

Raesh and Sarinda hurried back into the mountain. Sarinda took up a position at the entrance to the apartments, allowing Raesh to rush to his and Andie's apartment for what he needed. It didn't take him long to find it. It had never been moved since they placed it there.

He came hurrying back out only to find that the danger was over and Sarinda had defeated the final soldier. They took the train back down, though it barely survived to get them back to the main hub. From there, they rejoined the fight, pushing forward to the front of the University.

Still, the sheer numbers of the army were overwhelming and they had their work cut out for them. The army wasn't made of true soldiers any more than the professors were. Apart from Raesh, Sarinda, and the council fighters, the battle was evenly matched. Luckily, once they pushed forward far enough, Raesh and Sarinda made it to one of the hidden passages built for such an occasion. It was a dark, winding path that cut through the mountainside, but at least they had a break from the onslaught. Once they reached the end, they got an unwelcome surprise. The passage wasn't complete.

The exit was never made because the army arrived a whole week ahead of time.

"Great," Sarinda said. "Just what we need."

"I've got a spell for this," Raesh said, already raising his free hand.

"Yeah, I know, and I've got a couple. But we don't know what we're going to run into out there. If we just go blasting through the side of the mountain, we could end up right in the middle of them, surrounded."

"Well, we can't just stand here. So, either we go back and try to keep pushing to the front doors, which could take all night and I'm sure the front doors are even more heavily guarded, or you can help me blast through dirt and stone and we take our chances on the other side."

"Obviously, that's not much of a choice."

Raesh shrugged. "Here goes nothing."

The two raised their hands and began blasting their magic against the earth in front of them. They pushed and released with all they had, and fortunately they were not far from the end. But as soon as they found daylight, they also found themselves right in the middle of a dense crowd of soldiers.

Sarinda sighed. "Told you so."

Just quick enough to avoid a shotgun blast, Sarinda whipped the wind around herself and Raesh, knocking all the soldiers far back. They took advantage of the opportunity to head down the mountain toward the train. Spells and bullets and projectiles flew, exploding into the ground at their feet and blowing huge chunks of earth into the air. Raesh and Sarinda ran so fast they almost tripped going down the slope, casting and ducking as they went. They finally reached level ground and headed for the train, only the commotion they caused seemed to have attracted the attention of virtually all the soldiers stationed outside of the University.

"I'm really doubting our plan now!" Sarinda called.

"We can make it!"

But before they could even get within a reasonable

distance, more soldiers appeared and came together in front of them. Raesh and Sarinda paused, turning in every direction looking for an escape, but they were surrounded.

Raesh raised his hand and cast a spell. A massive byzantium purple ray of light shot up into the air, so powerful it made him stumble. The light shot up into the cloud, and Raesh maintained it for as long as he could before he had to go back to defending himself.

"Super pretty light," Sarinda said. "Want to tell me what it was for?"

"Just desperation."

"Can that thing you're carrying help us or is it just for Andie?"

"Just for Andie, I think."

"Come on, back to back."

Once again, they found themselves pressed upon and threatened. They parried and reflected, stringing out the inevitable end that awaited them. They were surrounded by more men than they could count, and each was doing his utmost to destroy them. When the bullets began to fly among the spells again, Sarinda clapped her hands above her head and a shield came down around them. She knew she couldn't hold it forever, not with so many attacking them at once.

But she only needed to hold it for a few seconds.

The first thing that happened was that a terrifying roar was heard. It was followed by four more. Within moments of the fantastic roars, five gargantuan dragons came soaring up over the precipice and swooped down over the soldiers there. The dragons opened their great jaws and spewed flames over the soldiers. The army scattered, every man running for his life, screaming as they abandoned the attack.

The dragons continued to spray fire until every man was cleared or burnt to a crisp. The creatures landed, and it was mere moments before Andie was in Raesh's arms. They both had never felt so relieved.

"So, you saw my distress signal," he said, still holding her.

"It was hard to miss."

She released him and then went to hug Sarinda.

"A few minutes later and we'd have been done for," Sarinda said.

"I was just waiting for a glorious entrance."

"Saeryn, it's good to see you back safe," said Raesh.

"It is good to be back. I'm only sorry we lost four of our own along the way. How have you fared here?"

"Well, we haven't really. The army got here a week ahead of schedule and we were completely caught off guard. We barely managed to get everyone to safety in time. But when we heard over the radio that you were back and that you were fighting, everybody found their courage. They're mounting an attack inside right now."

"No," Andie said. "They got into the University?"

"Yeah. We thought everyone would be safe in there and that it was impenetrable or at least would require a few days of siege, but one minute it was totally quiet and the next we were being overrun."

"The portal," Andie said, turning to Saeryn to confirm. "They're coming through the portal in Leabharlann. We were flying all over Noelle trying to track them down. But we know for a fact that the Dead have at least two. They must have set them up wherever they made camp and used them to cut the distance and get here earlier."

"And with the portal in Leabharlann they got to skip security and come right in."

"Is everybody safe? In the University or in a shelter?"

"Yeah. The city is completely empty."

"Good. Then we need to close that portal now."

"Come on. There's a secret entrance over here."

They hurried over to the exploded hole in the mountain where Raesh and Sarinda exited. They had to blast their way back in from where the opening collapsed. Raesh went down first, followed by Saeryn. Andie rushed up behind them and leapt into the hole.

She turned to look behind her and lost her breath.

A battalion soldier had snuck up on them and caught Sarinda by her throat. He held her in the air, as if her weight were nothing. With his free hand, he broke one of her arms and then held the other hand so she couldn't cast. Andie raised her hand to cast her spell, but just as her hand raised level with her face, the soldier flicked his wrist and Andie heard Sarinda's neck break.

For a moment, she was unable to think. Raesh sent a spell past her head and caught the soldier in his chest. It knocked him off his feet, but he rolled and got up again. But no sooner had he stood again than Andie raised her fist toward him and opened her fingers wide. He disintegrated on the spot. Andie's eyes grew wide as Raesh whistled in response. She didn't even know she was capable of such a thing.

Andie ran back out to Sarinda. She took her head in her hands and tried to wake her, but she was gone. There was no life left in her eyes.

"No," Andie said softly. "No."

Saeryn came back out and grabbed one side of Sarinda, indicating that Andie should grab the other. It took Andie a moment to focus, but then she lifted her ally, her friend, and they carried her into the mountainside. They both carried her along through the tunnel, Andie hardly able to see anything through the darkness and her tears. They arrived in the University and made their way to the main hub. They could still hear intense fighting going on in the distance, but the professors and council fighters had managed to push the army far back. Andie and Saeryn lay Sarinda down near the edge of the room. They and Raesh sat next to the body and mourned.

THE ENGINEERS HAD FINISHED their work on the battalion suits and Ashur was ready to lead his forces into battle. They did not have the natural ability of the Dead, but they were certainly not a force to be trifled with. They were one of the most formidable and dangerous armies to march those lands in living memory. No one truly knew the limits of their power. Lucas stood ready and alert, prepared to follow his commander into the most brutal and bloody wars of recent memory. All the soldiers shared that loyalty, that undying obsession to serve Ashur in any and every way possible. Such brainwashing was part of their training.

Ashur stood at the front of his battalion. He was only twenty-seven years old, but already he carried enough anger and hate in his veins to fill a hundred lifetimes. Large parts of his old armor merged with his flesh, and he wore a newer, stronger armor over that. His training was unimaginable, his desire unshakeable, his fury and his power undeniable. He had waited and waited for this day, his revenge on those who he felt had falsely taken up a residence in his world.

In his mind, there was only room for one leader, and it must be him. His face was terribly disfigured, half melted by the bolt from that despicable dragonborn Andie Rogers that nearly killed him. His body ached in constant pain. His mind twisted in part by insanity and part by the blinding need for revenge. But what he was capable of was both great and horrifying. Even Beladorion had underestimated him.

Without any pomp or circumstance, he gave the order and his men began to file toward the portal.

CHAPTER NINETEEN

"No. No, we're not going to do this. We can't afford to. Not now."

As she spoke, Andie got to her feet and pulled Raesh up with her. Saeryn stood, too, though all looked shaken and unsteady.

"Sarinda was brave and strong and she doesn't deserve this," Andie continued. "But we can mourn for her later. We have so much work to do, beginning with shutting down that portal."

Raesh nodded and all three hurried toward Leabharlann. They reached the library and rushed across the room to the Archives. Down and through they went until they reached the portal. Just as they entered the room, a battalion soldier emerged, followed by another, and another. Saeryn didn't even allow them the chance to raise their hand. She waved her arms in an inward sweep and the sand and dirt from the floor were brought up into a localized storm, picking the soldiers up and slamming them into the ground so hard Andie was sure they must have been pulverized. But, surprisingly, they stood. They marched forward again, and more were still coming.

"Upgrades," said Andie.

The three together began casting with ferocious speed and power. Raesh's pearlblood magic knocked the soldiers right back through the portal. Andie lifted the stone floor beneath the soldiers' feet and folded it over backwards, crushing them back into the portal. Saeryn's blade put down two soldiers. Once the room was clear, Andie rushed to the portal and recalibrated it. One soldier was caught half way between destinations and was promptly cut in two.

As the soldiers were thrown back through, barely alive, Ashur was surprised. One soldier looked through the portal and only the bottom half of him fell to the ground when it changed. Lucas, still standing beside the portal, looked completely baffled.

"My leader… I was sure… I thought…"

"Never mind, Lucas," Ashur said. "This is not your fault. It's the dragonborn. This is what they do. Maim and destroy. It doesn't matter. We'll just have to adapt our plans. Recalibrate it to follow the Dead. We'll land in Arvall and then attack."

ANDIE STEPPED BACK from the portal and breathed in relief. With the battalion's plans to enter through Leabharlann stopped, they had one less thing to worry about. Raesh stepped forward, looking down into the portal.

"I thought we were going to turn it off?" he asked. "At least it looks like there is no sign of the time curse. Doesn't stop the enemy from using it to transport across our own time, though."

"Yeah. Not just the enemy. But I almost forgot… Hang on."

And without warning, she jumped into the portal. Raesh rushed up and leaned over the surface of the device, so shocked he hadn't even calmed down enough to be afraid. Saeryn came up behind him and laid a hand on his shoulder, her face frozen in a look of shock as strong as Raesh's. Together, they waited and watched, but it was only a matter of moments before Andie resurfaced. And she was not alone.

With her came Yara and a handsome, intelligent-looking young man with blond hair and green eyes. Bonhaus. Raesh had a moment of absolute disbelief before he finally believed his eyes and embraced Yara.

"But you're dead!" he said.

"Not as dead as I could be. It's so good to see you," Yara said. She then turned to Andie and frowned. "I was starting to think maybe you weren't coming."

Andie shook her head and smiled. "I'm sorry. But you're here now."

Raesh was still frozen in shock. "I know we don't have the time right now, but someday soon you're going to have to tell me how it's possible for you to be here."

"I will, I promise. Everybody, this is Bonhaus."

"Hi," Bonhaus said, in a strong voice.

Yara paused for a moment and looked at Andie.

"Raesh," Yara started again. "You should know that Bonhaus is—"

"The man you love," Andie finished.

The two girls shared a look and then a smile. And just like that the bond was renewed.

Raesh scratched his head and turned to Andie. "But, how did you... Where did she... I don't..."

"Another time," Andie placed her hand on Raesh's shoulder and smiled. "I'm sure Yara has a lot to catch us up on her own adventures, but for now we must focus on our own."

"From the looks of you three I'd say we're already under attack," Yara said.

"They're here a week before we thought was

possible. They're using the portals to travel faster. I'm shutting this one down now," Andie said, turning the portal off in some capacity, so that at least the enemy couldn't come through from the other side. "But they can still get in by the one down in the city. Our main concern now is to push the enemy out of the University and reclaim this as a safe haven."

"Let's go. Bonhaus and I are ready. We've been ready and waiting for a very long time. I'm just sorry more of us weren't around when you finally came through to find me, Andie. Does anybody know how Carmen's doing?"

Now Andie paused. She had forgotten that Yara hadn't seen her friend in months, not since that day in the Hot Salts of Mithraldia when the dragon carried her away.

"She's awake," Raesh said.

Both Andie and Saeryn turned their heads toward Raesh. Andie advanced on him.

"What?" she asked. "Since when?"

"Since a couple of days ago. I wanted to let you know, but I couldn't reach you. She's awake and she's strong and when this is all over you can both see her. She's in The Letter, in Taline."

A flood of relief and joy came over Andie as she stood there, her knees threatening to give out beneath her from shear elation. Before she knew what was happening, she and Yara were hugging again, rejoicing in the news they'd waited so long for.

"But as long as we're doing updates, there's more, and I'm afraid it's bad. Yara, you don't know, but we just lost Sarinda. And for all of you, we've lost Professor Iceubes and Oren."

"What?" Saeryn said, her hand moving up to her chest. "When? How?"

"The Dead attacked your home in the Hot Salts. They've captured all of your people who were there at the time, but they haven't killed them. They only killed Oren. He wouldn't stop defending your people. He took down his share of Dead before they got him."

Andie, Saeryn, and Yara were all heartbroken. It hurt that much worse when great news was followed by terrible. For the first time, Andie saw Saeryn's brave face falter. Tears threatened to spill from her lids, and it was no wonder. Oren had been one of her truest friends and strongest allies. Andie didn't know which made her feel guiltier. That Oren died because he had to defend their people alone, or that Professor Iceubes died performing a task she gave him. Ultimately, she knew it no longer mattered. She could pity them and herself later. They had to keep going. They had to save the city.

"Okay," she said. "Okay, okay. We've suffered some losses. Heavy and early. But this war isn't over. It's only just getting stated. All of us need to get to the hallway now. We're the strongest fighters here and now is not the time to fall apart, no matter how weak we feel."

There were some halfhearted nods and the wiping of eyes. Everyone breathed. Bonhaus rubbed Yara's back for comfort. Andie took a breath and then turned to hurry back out to the hall.

When they reached the fighting, the professors rallied at the sight of them, parting to let them to the front. Armed with the heartache of their losses, the new group that Andie led cast spells more powerful and devastating than any that army had ever seen.

All through the hall, soldiers were falling or fleeing, terrified of the newcomers whose fury far outweighed their own. Andie, Saeryn, and Raesh worked as a perfect unit, casting and slicing their way toward the front of the University. Just left of them, Yara and Bonhaus were no mean feat, either. Despite his lithe form and handsome looks, Bonhaus fought like he was born to it, mixing casting and hand to hand combat in a seamless blend. He was stronger than he looked, smart, and lethal. Beside him, Yara was a force of nature, demonstrating all the things she learned from Andie and the new tricks she'd picked up on the eastern shores of Noelle. Andie also noticed a new strange flare to her magic, one she must have picked up from wherever and whenever she had ended up on the other side of the portal when Oren sent her through. She would have to ask more about that place when they had more time. Andie was just fortunate she was able to use the portal to their own advantage while they still had it, and that the time curse didn't somehow send her back in time when she jumped to get Yara and Bonhaus.

The army tried to maintain some sense of dignity, but the close space and the fury of Andie and her team unnerved them to the point where they could no longer take it. One of the soldiers called for a retreat and suddenly the whole mass fled. Andie had half a mind to shoot spells into their backs, but she was heavy with the thought of what had already been lost. She let them run for their lives.

She continued forward until she came out of the University's front doors. The mercy she showed had only spared a few, for no sooner were the men outside than the dragons began to spray fire again. Saeryn called to the dragons to calm them, her soft song carrying in the wind. The mountain side was alive with scrambling soldiers racing down the slopes. It would take them all night and part of the morning to finally reach the bottom.

A cheer went up through the professors and students. They had finally reclaimed the University, but Andie knew the battle was far from won. The men would regroup at the base of the mountain and join the rest of the army. The battalion would launch its attack.

The Dead, who were hiding somewhere among the buildings, would seek their revenge. Blood would be shed, and much of it.

Amidst the celebrations, the dragons began to call out. It almost sounded as if they were hurt. Andie and Saeryn rushed to them and tried to calm them, but they were inconsolable. The celebrations dwindled as all heads turned to the dragons, who were growing more and more agitated.

"What's wrong with them?" Andie asked.

"I've only ever seen them react this way once," Saeryn said, taking a nearby dragon's head in her hands. "It is how they react when one of their own is suffering."

"But I don't understand, there aren't any dragons up here. I know they can sense each other, but wouldn't they need to at least be within a few kilometers of each other?"

"The city," Saeryn said. "If the Dead are here they surely brought our people as their captives. And they're dragons, too. They would want them near to make sure they could not escape and to have ready access to their blood once the spell is broken. We must go now."

Saeryn leapt up onto the dragon and Andie climbed up behind her.

"What can we do?" Yara asked.

"Nothing," Andie said. "The only way to get there

fast enough is to fly down on the dragons. We'll be back as soon as we can."

The dragons lifted off and plunged down the mountainside, as fast as Andie had ever seen them fly. In mere seconds, they passed the soldiers who fled from the University. Down and down the dragons flew in a slanting dive, racing to their brothers' and sister' aid. They flew so fast and purposefully that Andie had to hold on tight or risk being lost. After a very brief time, the dragons reached the bottom and leveled out, shooting into the city and down the streets like enormous, breathing bullets. The force of the wind rushing past was so strong and loud that Andie couldn't even hear the dragons' wings beating.

Finally, Andie saw the dragonborn prisoners ahead. She could hardly believe when the dragons found a way to go even faster. Andie could see roughly a dozen Dead standing guard. She hoped the dragons would aid them in taking out the Dead, but instead the dragons simply landed and sat, their enormous forms frozen in place somehow.

Andie couldn't believe it. Saeryn didn't seem surprised. They both dismounted and drew their swords. The Dead began to circle in that flashing way of theirs and Andie wasted no time. She targeted the locks of the cages with her magic and closed her hands. At least a hundred cages were instantly opened and the dead were outnumbered. The Dead grouped together and stared at the dragonborn, contemplating their next move. They grimaced, unhappy to be taken by surprise. Andie targeted more locks and crushed them, too. And all the free dragonborn raced to free their people and their dragons. The Dead knew better than to fight now. They turned and ran.

Andie and Saeryn joined the others and continued taking the locks off the cages. Their people laughed and cried to have their freedom again. As soon as they were all free, Saeryn urged them to mount their dragons and fly up to the University. The streets vibrated with the sound and force of so many wings beating up into the sky. Andie and Saeryn were last, making sure they had freed every last one of their people.

Andie couldn't help trying to delude herself that Oren might still be there, waiting for them to save him. She and Saeryn mounted up and took off. But they were only in the air for a few moments before Andie saw something. Saeryn must have seen it, too, because she turned the dragon in the very direction Andie stared. A large group were coming toward the city from the direction of the String Fields.

Andie was still too far away to see clearly, but they weren't moving in any formation she had seen before, not of the battalion or the army. They moved at a moderate pace, so they were not of the Dead either. The dragon landed just in front of them. They'd already stopped moving when they saw the creature flying toward them. Andie observed them before getting down. They wore dark clothes, heavy boots, bags and crates marked "Explosive," not to mention a smell of extreme cleanliness, their scent pungent in the crisp air.

"You're from the mine cities in the north," Andie said.

"Yes, ma'am," one of the men said. "Are you Princess Andryne or Queen Saeryn?"

"I'm Andie. This is Saeryn. What are you doing so far from home?"

"Well, if you'll pardon the intrusion, a few months back me and my wife found a young girl in pretty bad shape. We took her in got her back on her feet and she stayed with us a while until she figured out what she wanted. Then she left. Well, truth be told, she made quite an impression on me and my wife and we told her she could call on us for anything, any time. Then a few days ago, we get a call telling us she's part of a revolution and they need as many hands as they can get as fast as they can get. She explained everything to us.

"I don't know how much you know about the cities in the north, but we never liked the University. They've been stealing from us and keeping us poor for too many cycles to count. And we never hated you or your people. You've never done anything to us. But more than all of that, when Yara called and said she needed our help, we came directly down and we brought our explosives, too."

The mining cities in the north were famous for their explosives and combustible mixtures. They were also noted builders and refiners, and a people tougher than the steel they used to excavate.

"We spread the word through the towns and everyone came when they could. We've been gathering in your neighbor city and when everyone got here, we came the rest of the way on foot. We're ready. Put us to work."

CHAPTER TWENTY

THE MINERS CAME IN A GROUP OF JUST OVER ONE thousand, a number that could go a long way in changing the outcome of the war. They had also brought enough powerful explosives to blow up Arvall three times over. Andie and Saeryn talked with them and made a plan for a coordinated attack. Andie warned them to stay out of the city until nightfall to protect themselves from the Dead, and then she gave them the locations of shelters that still had available space. They set a plan for the next day before Andie and Saeryn left for the University.

Once they reached the school again and were inside, the first person Andie ran into was Lymir. He threw his arms around her as she approached.

"Aye, we've missed you around here, girl," he said.

"You, too, Lymir."

Raesh and Yara came running up, their expressions ecstatic.

"We've got news," Raesh said. "The Thabians radioed us from their ships. They're on their way to Arvall. They're coming to help us and they'll be here by morning. They asked us to call them back with our attack plan."

"We've got news, too," said Andie. "We ran into some people from the mining cities in the north. Friends of yours, I believe," she said, looking at Yara. "There's about a thousand of them and they brought all the explosives we'll ever need. I've spread them throughout the city."

"This war might finally be looking up for us."

"Well, don't stop enjoying the good news yet," said Lymir. "As long as surprise forces are coming to our aid, I might as well tell you that the forces I've stashed all over the city will be ready tomorrow, too. No one's been able to get an accurate count yet, but I'd say we have a fighting chance now."

"My only concern are the Dead," said Saeryn. "They will not go quietly. They have been waiting centuries for the chance to obtain our power. It will be the defining battle of our people. I ask that, if at all possible, the rest of you avoid confronting the Dead. They will hunt my people out on the battlefield and my people are best equipped to handle them."

"What shape are they in? Will they be able to fight?"

"With a little food and rest, they'll be ready by morning."

"The dragonborn can all ride their dragons down to the city, but what about the rest of us?" Yara asked. "How are we supposed to get our forces down to Arvall in time to launch a coordinated attack?"

"We'll use the portal," Raesh said. "By now everyone who's coming through to the city is here. It should be safe to use."

"We need to get everyone together," Andy said. "The Thabians and the miners are going to be waiting for our signal in the morning and we need to have our plan down. I think for this the Grand Mirror Hall will do. Let's spread the word."

They all turned and began heading for the largest of the mirror rooms, the Grand Mirror Hall of Terpsichore. Everybody went ahead except Lymir, who stopped in the hall and placed his hand on the intercom system that was usually used for the siren's call. Using his magic, he connected his voice to the intercom and urged every person who planned to fight with them in the morning to make their way to the Grand Mirror Hall. Aside from the main hub, it was the only room in the University that could hold so many people at once. Lymir asked that everybody who was not going to fight look after the wounded and try to clear the halls and tunnels of any blockage.

In the Grand Mirror Hall, the people poured in. The room was completely empty and, in fact, hadn't been used since Chancellor Mharú killed the diplomats the night the dragonborn arrived in their world. But now the people rushed in, filling all the available space. They seemed much better now, more excited and hopeful. Winning the small victory in the University had done more for their morale and determination than any speech could have.

Andie, Raesh, Yara, Bonhaus, Saeryn, and Lymir all stood on a bare platform Saeryn had conjured. When the room held as many people as it could, the spectators began to quiet down as they looked up to their leaders. Andie and the others on the platform looked back and forth among each other, trying to decide who would speak. Somehow, the silent consensus gave the honor to Andie. She took a last look at Lymir, head of the University, and Saeryn, Queen of the dragonborn, to make sure it was not overstepping her bounds. When they all bowed their head to her, she stepped forward.

"I want to thank each and every one of you for what you've done today. I know it was only a small victory, but you fought hard and showed the enemy that if they want this city they need to be willing to die for it. Because we are. And to the dragonborn, I'm so happy to have you back here, safe and among friends. I only wish we had found you sooner. We took a big step in getting back our courage today and I'm proud.

"But this war has only begun. We've flown over some of the enemy strongholds down in the city and it looks as if they're prepared for a full siege. It could last days. Our enemies are many. There is the army made up of hundreds of different factions from all over Noelle, but also more dangerous foes. The Church of Stone and Sea has weaponized the red sand, combined with its other abilities, and they've marched against us. The battalion has returned, stronger, more full of hate, and lead by Ashur—trained by the Chancellor himself—and they march against us. A very old, very powerful enemy has risen from the shadows. The Beautiful Dead, descendants of the dragons and sworn enemy of myself and my people. Their physical abilities are astounding and incredibly dangerous, and they march against us. The enemy outnumbers us and they have some pretty terrifying abilities.

"But we have not been abandoned. Lymir has been training a force in secret and they're ready to fight with us tomorrow. The Thabians are sailing to us from the True Isles with their incredible weapons, and the miners have come down from the north with more explosives than we could use in a lifetime. And the dragonborn have been rescued, and when they're rested they and their dragons will fight as well. And everyone you see here onstage will be down in the city giving the battle everything we have.

"Tomorrow, at dawn, we're going down to war. Lymir and I will coordinate our allies and forces throughout the city. The dragonborn will fly down the mountain on their dragons and lead the attack. The rest of you will go down on EARTH 1. Let me explain. I went to the city transport department after we defeated the Chancellor and asked them to begin constructing an underground train from the city to here in case of emergencies. That giant dome at the foot of the mountain that everybody thinks is a fertilizer plant is actually the construction site. They finished building about a month ago. I didn't tell anyone except Lymir and Saeryn. I wanted to play it close to the vest. EARTH 1 is faster than SKY 6 and can get you to the base of the mountain in half the time. It can also hold more people. I think two trips should be enough to get everybody down. The best part is no one will be expecting it and that's exactly what's going to win us this war. The element of surprise. The enemy has no idea that we have allies coming, that we have men stashed throughout the city, or that we have EARTH 1. And they certainly won't be expecting what I have planned for SKY 6. None of us will be riding that.

"Right now, I want you all to eat and get some rest

because beginning at dawn we're going to be at war in earnest."

Andie took a step back and watched the people as they filed out of the room. It took a while because there were so many, but the people were in a rush to get themselves ready and to rest. Lymir left, too, to get on the radio with his secret forces. The dragonborn were the last to leave, taking a few last moments to look on their Queen and princess. Andie tried to hold on just a little longer. Finally, she saw him. Gordenson, chief physician of the dragonborn. She motioned for him and he came smiling, as happy to be safe and among friends as Andie was to have him. He came to a stop just in front of her and she gestured for him to wait. When the last person left the room, Andie let herself go. She fell backward, but Raesh was there to catch her. Yara, Bonhaus, and Saeryn crowded around her. Gordenson knelt beside her.

"Princess," he said. "What's happened?"

"The Dead," she said. "We ran into them in southern Noelle. The Black Grotto. Saeryn and I were the only ones who escaped, but we didn't get out unscathed. The Dead have special daggers. Wherever they cut us, our bodies refuse to heal."

"Wrothsaield," said Bonhaus. "It's the name of their blades. Yara and I came across it in our research. The blades are made of cursed metal, no one is sure exactly what kind. Part of the curse was to infuse the blades with the blood of the first Dead who wielded them. Those daggers can cut through anything, even dragon hide if they wanted to."

"One more thing to worry about," said Andie.

"The blades were cursed because they were made for a special purpose. To break the spell and allow the Dead to take on the magic of the dragonborn. All they need to do is plunge the blades into the hearts of all the living descendants of the man who paced the spell on them."

"So that's it," Saeryn said. "That's how they'll do it."

"Yeah, that's not happening," said Raesh.

"I hate war," Andie said. "How does it look Gordenson?"

The physician tore the top of Andie's shirt to examine the cut.

"It's starting to become infected, but I can clean it for you. The one on your cheek isn't too bad, but the one on the back of your hand is all the way to the bone. Thank goodness you did such a job wrapping it or you would have bled out hours ago. I can treat the wounds and stitch them. Your dragon blood won't heal these, but your body will, at a normal rate. I haven't seen wounds like these since the old days."

"Well, as soon as you're done with me, see to the Queen, too. These cuts hurt like you wouldn't believe."

"You'll tear your stitches fighting tomorrow," Raesh said.

"No, she won't," said Gordenson. "I'll spell the stitches to move as she moves. It'll still hurt, but it won't interfere with the healing process."

"Okay. Thank you," Andie said. "Since I'm going to be here for a while, Yara I need you and Bonhaus to get on the radio and coordinate the miners. They should have reached the shelters by now. Make sure everyone is eating and resting. You rest, too."

"I want to stay with you," Yara said.

"I not quite sick of you either," Andie said with a smile. "But there are very few people I trust to lead this fight. You're one of them. By extension, you, too, Bonhaus. So, please, help me out here."

Yara huffed a bit, but bent down to take Andie's hand for a moment, then she and Bonhaus hurried out. Gordenson went to get his bag and then he saw to Andie while Raesh held her. He also treated Saeryn's wounds. He gave them both something for the pain, something tailored especially for their dragon blood. Within moments, they felt better, though there was too much pain to be rid of it completely.

Andie and Saeryn got to their feet and they all made their way out of the mirror hall. They moved toward the main hub and there they found everybody eating and resting. They walked into the room and first there were smiles. But then there were gasps.

Andie turned around, moving Gordenson to the side with her arm so she could cast. There were six battalion soldiers standing in the hall. Four in the front and two behind.

"You must be on a suicide mission," Andie said.

"No exactly," one soldier said. "We were already in the Archives when you stopped the others. And now we're going to kill you."

"Now I know you're delusional."

"Let's see who laughing in ten seconds. Boys, camouflage."

The four soldiers in front tapped something on their wrists. But nothing happened. They tapped it again. Nothing happened. Now they began to panic. Andie was seconds from casting, but before she could send even one spell, the two soldiers in the back raised their hands and broke the backs of the four soldiers in front. The whole room went still. No one knew what is happening. Andie looked at the two soldiers, her hand still raised.

"Who are you?"

"Old friends," one of the soldiers said.

The soldiers took their helmets off. It was Kent and Lilja.

An hour later, Andie, Raesh, Saeryn, Lymir, Yara, Bonhaus, Kent and Lilja were rested and fed, as was everyone else. The forces were spread out through the University, sleeping, or not sleeping if they were praying or talking with their families. It was the first real moment of peace they'd had since they first got the news that the army was marching on the city. A peace before the calm. Kent and Lilja were broken when they heard about Sarinda, especially Lilja, who hadn't seen her since the day they split up in the Hot Salts of Mithraldia. Now she'd never be able to know if Sarinda forgave her or not.

Lilja and Kent had travelled to the Old World, the continent on the other side of the vast reach of the Spider Sea. They had been following a lead for Andie, based on information she'd gotten from Saeryn. During the first war with the University in Saeryn's time, many dragonborn families fled to the Old World to escape persecution. The University's power couldn't reach that far, and the dragonborn were safe there.

Weeks before she was pulled through the portal, Saeryn made a journey across the sea to convince her people to come home. Many of them did return, but a lot stayed behind, preferring to stay safe rather than to fight. Andie had charged Kent and Lilja months before with finding any dragonborn descendants on that side of the sea. Saeryn was sure none would have survived the curse that threatened to wipe her people out back in her original time—the curse she had called to Andie in the future to save them from—but she allowed them the chance to go investigate in case. To everyone's surprise, they had found some, but they were even less willing to fight than their ancestors.

Kent and Lilja journeyed all the way across the Old World and returned to Noelle from the east. From there, they began tracking the battalion, taking out as many as they could before finally disguising themselves and joining the ranks. The two climbed their way up. They'd both had engineer training and so they put their skills to use, working on the suits for the battalion and connecting them all to the same network. The enhancements for the suit were real, but Kent and Lilja installed new programming that allowed them to disable the suits remotely, just as they'd done to the four soldiers who tried to turn on their camouflage. They hadn't brought back the dragonborn reinforcements, but they had come home able to shut down the battalion's suits, leaving Ashur and his men with nothing but some very expensive pieces of clothing. The only catch was they didn't have the clearance to get access to a level of the network high enough to have a trickledown effect. They would need to capture either Lucas or Ashur and plug into their suit.

"Looks like we've got a few secret weapons after all," Raesh said, holding Andie.

By then, everyone else was asleep and Andie and Raesh curled up in a corner of the main hub, exhausted.

"It's still going to be a longshot," she said. "We have to coordinate all these groups perfectly."

"And fight. Are you ready?"

"I never have been. Never will be."

"Me neither."

"So... we don't need to have one of those emotional and uncomfortable conversations about our feelings, do we?"

"Nope. I know how you feel about me."

"Good. I know how you feel about me, too."

CHAPTER TWENTY-ONE

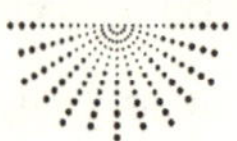

THE NEXT MORNING, RAESH FINALLY GAVE ANDIE THE thing he brought from their apartment. It was her armor. They were outside, in front of the University, surrounded by all the professors, students, and citizens who chose to fight with them. The dragonborn were there, too, beside their dragons, their hands on the hilts of their swords. Saeryn, Gordenson, Lymir, Yara, Bonhaus, Kent, Lilja, and even Murakami were there. Andie had never put the armor on before. She has been afraid of it and of the terrible things she might do inside of it. But a look from Raesh and Saeryn reassured her. She nodded and Raesh and Saeryn helped her put it on.

The armor fit perfectly. The smooth contours of the scaled metal fit her muscles and curves as if it were cut from her very own body. It felt incredible. In her head, Andie couldn't think of any way to describe it other than that it felt like home. The dragon scales glistened and changed color in the sun, and there must have been some powerful, beautiful magic flowing through it because she felt stronger, braver. Or maybe it was simply being surrounded by so many friends and allies in that short, rare moment of peace.

She tried to hold back the tears, but gave up and let them fall. She knew they were good, not tears of shame or weakness, but tears of joy and pride. She looked around her at all the hopeful faces that looked back. She knew how much they were depending on her. She was just shy of twenty-four years old and never completed even one year of higher magical academic training, yet she and the Queen of her people were about to lead a force into war.

The people around her were hoping, praying she could save them, and she understood just then what Saeryn had been trying to tell her since the day they met. Being a Queen was sometimes about making difficult choices and sometimes about playing executioner, but it was always about protecting your people, no matter the sacrifice to yourself. Andie felt the burden take hold of her as she witnessed every emotion passing over the faces of the crowd around her. She was surrounded by everyone and everything living in the world that mattered to her. And it was time to protect it.

A path cleared for her to a dragon. Andie gasped when she recognized the beautiful creature. It was Ronen, Oren's dragon. Ronen met her gaze as she gazed into the stunning emerald depths of the dragon's eyes. A single tear formed in the dragon's eye, and Andie stepped forward to gently wipe it away. She placed her hand on Ronen's neck, and the creature craned her head to press against Andie's side.

Saeryn went first and mounted up. Andie turned to face her people, more determined than ever, and the people reached out to touch her as they crowded around. Something happened to her as she stood there, looking out over her people and the beautiful dragon who had lost her life-long companion. Something changed. She realized, for the first time with any true gravity, that she may never return. She thought to herself that that was okay, so long as the city and everyone in it were safe. She reached the dragon and turned to Raesh. She kissed him as if the war were over and they were staring into the face of a lifetime of peace.

"You still good on that conversation?" he asked.

"Yeah. You?"

"Still good." He smiled.

Andie levitated up into the air to see the crowd. She had never been prouder.

"I have only one thing to say to you," she called out. "So long as you can, fight."

With that, she settled onto Oren's beautiful green dragon, and all of the dragonborn rose into the air as one. Andie watched as Raesh, Yara, Lymir, and all her friends disappeared beneath them. Then with a ferocious roar, Saeryn's new fierce green companion began its dive down the mountainside, with all the other dragons following. Their descent was strong, straight, true. The city rose before their eyes as the dragons dashed for the foot of the mountain. As they neared the bottom, Andie could see the train station was crawling with soldiers who were guarding the portal that Marcus set up. This was what she'd hoped for. She sent a byzantium ray of light into the air as a signal to Raesh up on the mountain. He'd know what to do.

The dragons reached the bottom of the mountain and leveled out, heading into the city. They sprayed fire down on the soldiers, and, even at their incredible speed, Andie could still hear them screaming. The dragons wove through the streets, throwing their full weight into the enemy army's makeshift bunkers and wrapping their great powerful jaws around the posts supporting the army's watchtowers. As they came around for another pass, some of the dragonborn dismounted and ran ahead to fight on foot, allowing their dragons to target the enemy as they please. Saeryn brought Ronen around for another pass through the streets, this time targeting the supplies the enemy has stockpiled along the streets for easy access.

After wiping out nearly all the visible supplies in the area, Saeryn brought the dragon high above the city to get a view of their surroundings. Andie could see the Thabians and the Thabian ships pulling into the city docks, hundreds of them racing into the city to attack the enemy from the western edge. She turned and saw a series of explosions going off in a very tight, precise pattern from the opposite side of the battle. The miners. The explosions made her think of the trap she had set the night prior.

When she met with the miner yesterday, they gave her some explosives to take with her. It was a small amount, but the man said they were the most powerful in Noelle. Perhaps even in all of Shaeyara. Andie and her friends loaded those explosives onto the train last night and cut the breaks. Her purple light in the sky was the go-ahead for Raesh to release SKY 6. Just as she turned to look, the train came barreling into the station unable to stop. It jumped the tracks, plowed through the crowd of soldiers, and collided with the train station.

The explosion was both magnificent and terrifying. The combustion blew the windows out along twenty blocks of the city. The smoke and flames rushed into the air and reached even higher than the tallest skyscraper. The sound of it was something no one would ever forget. The train station was irrevocably obliterated and all that was left of where the massive crowd of soldiers stood was a monumental crater. Andie did not relish that such violence and death were the result of her planning, but she knew she had to defend her people. What made her feel better was the sight of their forces rushing out of the white dome, having just gotten off EARTH 1.

Saeryn brought them down again and they took a survey of the city. Their secret forces and the miners had come up from the shelters to fight, and the enemy army looked unpleasantly surprised. The miners had explosions going off all along the eastern edge of the city, and, though it was hard to tell from where she was, she thought the Thabians had made quite an entrance on the other side. She and Saeryn did a last pass to burn up some more of the enemy's supplies and then they dismounted to fight on foot. They touched down just in front of some battalion soldiers and got to work.

The war had begun.

THE FIGHTING RAGED all day and night. From the moment they soared down over the precipice of the mountain, the dragonborn hardly had a chance to rest. The professors and students, too, had proven themselves beyond valorous, fighting until they thought they couldn't, and then fighting some more. The fighting covered the entire city, from the foot of the mountain to the northern edge of the city, and from the Spider Sea all the way across to the String Fields. The dragons swooped in to catch an enemy in their claws or teeth, and sprayed their fire when they could, but they had sat the fight out for the most part so as not to hurt the good fighters who were battling in such close quarters with the enemy.

The two armies went after each other with everything they had. The streets rang with the deafening sound of gunfire and screaming. The air was thick and brilliant from endless spells and hexes being hurled through space and glass. Colors and collisions of all kind flashed in the air and against buildings as the armies cast simultaneously. Buildings were shaken and some even collapsed as the expression of magic filled nearly every street of Arvall. The sun rose in the east beyond the fields and set in the west against the horizon made by the shimmering sea, and still the fighting raged on without stop, without mercy.

Many were wounded, some gravely so. Many were dead. Those who were wounded were dragged far enough out of the fray to safety, until they could rest and recover and then take to the streets again. In some parts of the city the fighting slowed as the armies cast across boulevards from their hiding places. In other places, the stench of death was overpowering as soldiers from both sides collided in a close, furious brawl for the city and its soul. There was even fighting inside the buildings as soldiers chased their enemy inside and upstairs. The destruction and hatred knew no bounds, no limits.

Andie and Saeryn fought side by side, so elegant and powerful that they were almost never hit, not even by the battalion. On the rare occurrence they were hit, it was only a momentary wound, for the dragon blood healed them quickly—though the wounds they sustained from the Beautiful Dead in the Black Grotto still pained them. To conserve the magic in their blood, they did as much fighting as they could with their swords, though it was truly a magnificent sight to see them effortlessly cast a spell that could take out a dozen men. Andie went from casting spells, to using her sword, to hand to hand combat, and back again. Andie's arm ached from swinging the sword so much, so wildly. A part of her conscious just wanted the fighting, the inevitable death, to be done with, and she knew Saeryn felt the same way. She also knew what she was doing was right. She continued protecting her people.

Raesh, Yara, and Bonhaus fought in close quarters all day. Raesh's pearlblood magic was as wild as ever, and during the battle it served him well. Most of the enemy had never even heard of pearlblood magic, let alone seen it in action. Bonhaus was at his best, mixing his superb combat skills with his precise casting abilities. Yara's capabilities had grown remarkably since the last time she faced the battalion. She brought with her now all kinds of spells and hexes she picked up during her self-imposed exile, but her most lethal method was fighting with her wind daggers, which cut and flew back simultaneously. She was fantastic and undeniable. She, Bonhaus, and Raesh could be found wherever the fighting was thickest.

The Thabians and the miners managed to keep the battle contained on both sides. Some soldiers tried to flee across the sea, but they couldn't break the line of the Thabians who, for all their disdain for modern technology, were such skilled fighters that not even the battalion could break their formation. Their weapons, crafted in their beautiful secluded isles, were strong, true, and deadly. Soldiers laughed to see their bow and arrows, but their laughter did not lasted long. The miners, though lacking training and even rudimentary military skills, proved themselves a great help. They spent the night laying out mines along the border of the String Fields, horrifying traps for any enemy so bold as to try to escape that way. They had weapons that created both far-reaching jets of flame and multiple combustions. They were also incredibly skilled at localizing fire and manipulating it to their will.

Kent and Lilja spent the day seeking out battalion soldiers. They knew they didn't have the strength, even combined, to take down Ashur, but if they could find and defeat Lucas, they'd be able to hack his suit and send a command through the battalion network to make all of the suits useless. They hunted down battalion members wherever they could. They could still shut down the suits of any battalion soldiers in their immediate vicinity, and their work went a long way in helping to even the playing field. Many had forgotten just how powerful the battalion suits were. Kent and Lilja had to give the battalion the impression that they were helping them, so the enhancements were real, initially, but they were programmed to return to normal function the minute they came through the portal.

Even functioning at a normal level, however, the battalion was still incredibly dangerous. They were already combat specialists months ago, but their time among the Dead made them even more lethal. Their suits amplified what they could do naturally, which essentially meant they didn't need to stop and rest, a considerable advantage in a battle that lasted days.

Though Ashur was not yet fighting, Lucas had been on the streets of Arvall since before even Andie. His training was impeccable, precise, deadly. He was molded by Ashur, the commander himself, and thus he felt no remorse or pity, only a thorough hatred for the dragonborn and anyone who sided with them. Many died by his hands.

Lymir and Murakami fought long and hard, despite their age. They moved from shelter to shelter, helping to protect those who could not protect themselves. They also got on the radio and called out positions and patterns, giving their forces the best possible chances. Between fighting in the streets and their broadcasts, Murakami and Lymir made sure the supplies of all the shelters were still good, and they organized scavenging missions for their forces to steal supplies from the enemy.

The council fighters were as strong as ever, fighting in formations and varying the patterns so the enemy couldn't learn them. Despite their high numbers, they fought as a single unit, one well-trained and powerful body. They, like everyone else, fought thinking of all they had lost because of motions the University set into play centuries ago. They fought thinking of all they knew they would have to sacrifice before this war was over. With magic, fists, and guns they moved through the city, giving the battle everything they had.

CHAPTER TWENTY-TWO

The war raged on. The Dead still hadn't shown their faces, but Andie knew they were simply waiting for the most opportune moment. Morning became day, day became night, and in the darkness the fighting continued. The city was lit by the deranged flight of a thousand perilous spells.

"You..."

"Seem.. ."

"To..."

"Have..."

"Lost..."

"Heart."

. . .

"WILL..."

"You..."

"Simply..."

"Watch..."

"From..."

"Safety?"

Beladorion turned slowly to the priests and looked down at them, so much smaller and less intimidating than himself. But he knew better than to compromise the plan.

"It almost sounds as if you question my courage," he said. "One might even think you question my ability. I would advise against that. I have not underestimated you and I would suggest you not underestimate me. I know exactly what this looks like, as if I fear the blood traitors and only want to face them when they're weakest. That is half true. My people and I have no interest in fighting, at least not for very long. I've realized we can take no glory from this battle whether the traitors are fresh or exhausted. All we want is to kill the Queen and princess and drink of them. It will not hurt our pride if we have to take them at their lowest. Our aim is to evolve. Still, fear not. These blood traitors are strong and when the sun comes out again in the morning it will rejuvenate them. The morning will also be the day that we have waited for. And then we will descend upon them."

"We... "

"Shall..."

"Go..."

"Down..."

"At..."

"Midnight."

"Six priests in robes against this army? You're either extremely brave or much more naïve that even I believed. I suppose I understand why this is personal for you. The traitor princess is the first person to ever escape from your clutches. It is a total embarrassment. Have your fun priests. I will watch from here."

"Just..."

"Watch..."

"For..."

"The..."

"Red..."

"Sand."

THE NIGHT WORE on and the hours fell away. The war shifted its way around the city, winding through the streets, its fronts changing. The thickest fighting breaking apart, the thinnest converging, the city fell to pieces everywhere. Whole buildings collapsed and fires raged too big and too numerous to be extinguished. There had been heavy losses on both sides and some streets were impassable because of the bodies, but neither side wavered in its resolve.

As the night wound to its close, to the point where it became yet again morning, Andie came to a shelter for water and a moment's rest. She was also listening to the radio for news of Raesh and her other friends on the other side of the city. As midnight struck, a kind of wave passed through her. She felt awkward for a moment, but the feeling passed. Having heard neither good nor bad news about Raesh, Andie cleared her head and rushed back outside. On the street, she found Saeryn, who seemed a bit woozy.

"Are you okay?" Andie asked.

"Yes. I believe so. It just felt as if something passed through me."

"Yeah, I felt it, too. I have no idea what it was. Maybe the De—"

Andie couldn't finish her sentence because she saw something coming in their direction. It must have been thirty blocks away, but it closed the distance fast. It was massive, wild, blasting the glass from the windows and sweeping cars along as it came. The closer it got, the more Andie could see its color. Red. It didn't take her long to realize that it was the red sand of the Church of Stone and Sea. They had finally joined the war in the streets.

"Oh, yes," Andie said. "I've been waiting for you. Saeryn, our friends from the church here look a little sad. Let's brighten them up."

"With pleasure."

Saeryn put her hands to her mouth and made a very distinct call. She and Andie then waited, watching the looming threat draw near. The massive cloud of red sand continued to come toward them, sweeping everything in the street along and causing terrible damage. It was almost upon them, fierce, sprawling, morphing before their eyes, a huge cloud of magical and deadly grains. Just as it bore down on them, fire and black smoke billowed into its face. Ronen and the other dragons had heard her call.

The dragons flew above the cloud and sprayed down some of its heaviest and hottest flame yet, the entire surrounding city was cast in a red glow. The cloud became a giant mass of red glass and fell, shattering across the street. Among the shards and chunks were six priests, badly burned yet still strong enough to regain their feet. They clearly weren't expecting such a welcome. Just like in the Church weeks prior, they began to come together to merge as one. Very calmly, Andie drew her sword and held the blade in the opposite hand. She whispered an incantation over the blade, her eyes closed and her mind focused. The six priests became one.

"Little princess," the multi-voice said. "We now give you the choice to—"

Andie threw her blade right into the middle of the face and it stuck between its eyes. The spell began to spill out from the sword and the face started to melt, turning into a dripping, steaming jelly before dissolving completely. Andie held out her hand and the sword returned to her. Simple, quick, effective. She and Saeryn turned and walk away.

IN TALINE, across Noelle from Arvall City, the third wave of the army arrived. There were far too many of them to arrive on the train, and so they descended on the city from above, parachuting down from the silver cliffs. When the citizens of Taline looked up and see two thousand men descending on them, they panicked. But Stefan was calm. He surmised that an army marching on Arvall from the north might detach a faction to march on his city as well, and he had been prepared for this moment for days. He had organized the city's small force and even reformed the council.

The army rushed through the streets of Taline, hungry for bloodshed and pillaging. It was true that Taline had not been back on its feet long and still has a long way to go before reclaiming its former glory, but the one thing they did have was Stefan. Stefan the Unkillable, he was called in the old days. He was very old and very powerful, and he loved one thing above all others. His precious Taline City. It was a shame the soldiers didn't know this.

Taline's standing army was very small, and Stefan

sent half of them to fight alongside their allies in Arvall city. But what the forces of Taline lacked in numbers, they made up for in training. They were originally trained to hunt and capture the terrorists who plagued the city years before. Because of the frequent attacks, there was little order and much chaos, and these men hardened themselves fighting some of the worst and most ruthless criminals in western Noelle. They were a force to be reckoned with, and Stefan had organized them flawlessly. No sooner did the men touch down than the forces of Taline ambushed them and delivered an attack worthy of record in every history book.

Stefan himself was also in the streets fighting like a young man, despite his more than two hundred years. His spellwork was the product of more than two centuries of rigorous training and discipline. Not one of the soldiers could even get close to him without being vaporized. Stefan was a kind man, but he showed no mercy to those who wished to destroy his city. His magic was great and terrible. And beside him, fighting as if she had never been hurt, was Carmen.

She was as beautiful and deadly as ever, moving quickly and dexterously through the invading army, cutting them down with ease. She and Stefan forced the soldiers back toward Bane, a two-thousand-foot-tall, sun-fueled, living structure capable of defending itself. As the enemy was pushed within its reach, Bane's loveglass windows lashed out and snatched the soldiers from the streets, delivering them to an agony that made them glad for the death it eventually delivered.

Stefan and Carmen fought viciously, alongside the other council members, defending the city and ensuring more soldiers didn't arrive in Arvall.

CHAPTER TWENTY-THREE

Saeryn stumbled first, then fell. Andie knelt to help her, though she didn't feel very strong herself.

"What was that?" Saeryn asked, her eyes scanning their surroundings wildly.

"I felt it, too," Andie said. Her body was consumed by a great weakness, as if her very magical essence had been torn from her body.

"What is happening?" Both women looked panicked, their bodies weakening by the second. They could not track the source of the attack, but both felt their magic and physical strength slowly extinguish like a dampening flame.

Before Andie could answer, she was knocked twenty feet back and into a concrete column. She had to lay there for a moment to catch her breath, but before she could, a bolt of lightning struck her, knocking her backward through the pillar. She could hardly open her eyes as she waited for the dragon blood to heal her.

"That one's mine," Ashur said, pointing to Andie. "You're more than welcome to the Queen."

Andie saw him now and she saw his accomplice: Beladorion. She guessed from his dress and suffocating arrogance that he was the leader of the Dead. Ashur made his way over to her and lifted her with one hand. He held her in front of him, giving her a long look at the irrevocable damage she'd done to his face.

"It's not a pretty sight, is it?" he asked.

He punched her with all his force and then cast an acid spell right in her face. The pain was blinding and Andie dropped to the ground in agony. She put her hand to her face and only managed to have her palm eaten away, too. Ashur came in for his next strike, and, as he leaned forward, Andie cast an explosion right into his chest. She was thrown, skidding across the concrete and Ashur was blasted up through the steel and concrete overhang of the building.

Across the street, Beladorion was beating Saeryn to within an inch of her life.

"You know, I never understood you traitors," he laughed. "All we want is to have what you have. It's not as if we need to drink all your blood, though of course now we'll bleed you dry simply out of spite. Generations upon generations of both our people could have been spared if you had only shared your birthright."

"If you were to obtain our power, you would destroy everything," Saeryn said, crawling away to give herself time to heal. "By denying you we have protected the world."

"You've only put off the inevitable," he said, kicking her across the intersection. "You've only angered us."

Saeryn looked to her left, her right, and down the street in front of her. Everywhere she looked the Dead were beating the life out of her people. The dragonborn fought bravely, but the Dead's natural and physical attributes were formidable. Andie saw the carnage as well. She looked over to Saeryn, wondering how they would survive.

IN OTHER PARTS of the city the tides were turning against the defenders of Arvall. Murakami and a large number of council fighters were killed in a magical bombing by the battalion. Lymir had been missing for hours. Yara and Bonhaus collapsed from exhaustion and had to be carried off for rest and water. Raesh was still fighting valiantly, but he was being cornered by a phalanx of fifty battalion soldiers. The miners had been pushed out of the east side of the city and some of them had even run across their own traps. The line of the Thabians had finally been broken.

The Beautiful Dead were gaining the upper hand on the dragonborn, who were simultaneously suffering from the same odd weakness that was affecting Andie and Saeryn. The battalion had strong-armed its way into a position of advantage. The defenders of Arvall lacked the numbers and they were beginning to lack the will. Andie and Saeryn were taking a terrible beating at the hands of Ashur and Beladorion, and it seemed the spell was only moments from being broken.

But all hope was not lost. Kent and Lilja had searched all day and night for him and now they had finally hunted him down. Lucas. He was standing behind the phalanx of battalion soldiers. They finally had him. They wasted no time, stealthily running up to him from behind. Lilja jumped up and landed a knee to the back of his head, a perfect blow that dazed him and brought him down. Kent fended off the soldiers as they rounded on him.

Lilja worked quickly, getting out her equipment and hacking into the suit. It didn't take long to work, but Lucas came around for a few seconds, just long enough to blast a hole through Kent's back. Lilja screamed; she drew her knife and plunged it into Lucas's chest, repeatedly. The battalion soldiers all looked confused as their power dwindled, leaving them with nothing but their own meager ability. Sensing the change, Raesh gathered his magic in a wild, unstable ball in his hands.

"Lilja, get down!" he screamed.

He released the magic, the energy, and blew the soldiers away. The shutting down of the battalion suits was a turning point. Without their advanced suits, the battalion soldiers lost both their power and their arrogance. However, they were still skilled sorcerers. The defenders of Arvall sensed the opportunity and drew their will for one last try.

ASHUR FINALLY REGAINED consciousness and slammed back into the street. Andie had recovered enough to regain her feet. She saw him and moved in his direction. He pulled a whip from his back and it began to glow green with some kind of magic Andie knew must be dangerous. She drew her sword.

Ashur snapped the whip, but Andie was quicker. She cut it off, only to find that it grew back. She began casting as she defended against the flying whip.

Ashur cast, too, though he was less precise than Andie.

They traded spells as if they were born to do only that. Ashur performed through rage and hate, Andie through necessity. The whip caught Andie's leg across her shin and snapped her bone. He snapped it again across her face. When the whip came around again, Andie dove to the side, replacing her original form with a magical ghosted shadow, allowing the whip to pass through. She walked right up to Ashur and swung her fist just as he realized his whip had gone through empty air and landed her punch. Ashur spun on his feet and Andie landed more blows. But soon he was squared again and they engaged in hand to hand. They were both skilled fighters, catching each other with incredible blows, but Ashur's armor made him stronger, faster. He slapped Andie and she went spinning through the air.

But she was tougher than he could have imagined. She was right back on her feet, throwing her sword with such force and accuracy that it went right through his thigh. As he screamed in pain, Andie got a running start and jumped, coming down with a spell that crushed Ashur into the ground. She turned her fist to stone and began to pound him mercilessly. But his new armor and the old that was melded to his skin had made him strong.

He opened his mouth and screamed, amplifying it

with a spell so that the sound came out in percussive rings. Andie was blown back. She cast a spell at Ashur that caused him to bleed inside. She didn't notice until the final two seconds were ticking away that he'd placed a grenade on her. She wasn't concerned, since fire couldn't hurt her, but this was no regular grenade. As it exploded, it sent a wave through her that completely drained her. She dropped.

Saeryn rallied against Beladorion. She felt herself weakening every moment, but still she pressed on. She had drawn her sword and dueled against him and his Wrothsaield blades. Her footwork and form were excellent and she cast a spell to make her faster, leveling the playing field.

"Very good, traitor," Beladorion said. "For a moment, I worried I was fighting a common rat."

"You forget your place, boy," said Saeryn. "You descend on us when we are weakest and think you have cause to be proud. What a shame to find the great Dead are merely frightened children."

Beladorion lunged, and, although Saeryn blocked his blade, he moved to throw his shoulder into her and knocked her across the street. She recovered just in time to stab the arm that reached for her throat. He screamed. Saeryn launched an assault, slicing him so fast and expertly that even Beladorion had trouble tracking her. He was able to protect his main arteries, but Saeryn had free reign with everything else. She cast a spell that snatched a pillar from its support position and slammed it into Beladorion, knocking him two blocks away. Two more Dead arrived to help their leader, but Saeryn beheaded them both on her way to Beladorion.

But he was waiting for her and as she neared him. He regained his feet and aimed a kick at her chest in a mere second, sending her flipping over backwards and colliding with the ground. In a flash, he was on top of her, digging his blade into her hand.

MEANWHILE, a group of battalion soldiers had found Andie. Ashur was still in the crater she had beaten him in, recovering. The grenade that went off on Andie was designed to instantly shrivel the adrenal glands, instantaneously ridding the body of adrenaline. Andie was too weak to even move a finger. Adrenaline played a large role in dragonborn healing, so it was taking her a while to get back on her feet. The ten soldiers held her up and took turns beating her, like only cowards would do. But every punch they landed only made her stronger. She was healing. Slowly, she felt herself coming back.

Soon Ashur was on his feet and he cast a spell at one of the soldiers that completely froze him. He kicked the boy over and his body shattered.

"What do you think you're doing?" he shouted. "She's mine! Mine!"

Andie spat a mouthful of blood on the ground. "Aw, that's so sweet. I didn't know you wanted me that badly, but if you insist..."

Ashur launched himself away just in time. Magic rushed from Andie's body in an explosion of fire and lava. She was filled with such rage and such fury, she felt a renewed energy flood her veins, and she used it to its full potential. The other nine soldiers were burned away instantly. Ashur managed to escape, but his leg was badly burned. He struggled to his feet, but Andie pushed the wind between them with such force that he was thrown up at an angle, smashing through to the twelfth floor of a building and landing inside. Andie levitated up to the floor. Ashur was insensible on the floor and Andie kicked the arm he was trying to push up on, breaking it. He screamed in pain.

"I can't believe you were dumb enough to come back," she said. "You barely escaped with your life last time. Why would you test me?"

"And who are you supposed to be? An orphan? A prey? A lovesick imposter, pretending these people will ever actually love you? You disgust me."

Andie turned her hand and broke all his ribs. He screamed in agony.

"Trust me," she said. "The feeling is mutual."

But Ashur's scream of pain morphed into a deranged laughter. Andie grew uncomfortable. She began to cast again, but in the space of a second his armor pulsed blue and then exploded in a wave of energy that sucked the solar radiation right out of Andie. She collapsed. Ashur got to his feet. He didn't say a word, just walked up to her and kicked her so hard she went flying out of the window. She collided with the glass of the other building across the street, then fell.

* * *

BELADORION SWUNG his quick and powerful fist at Saeryn, but instead of connecting with her flesh, he hit metal. Saeryn had transformed her body to steel as best she could, though her memory of the spell in the grimoire grew faint in her battered head. She swung a punch of her own and sent Beladorion flipping and tumbling across three blocks. The blow was so hard the other Dead along the street stopped to look. The dragonborn, though still weak, had begun to rally. They started pulling out the best and strongest spells they knew, and wielded their swords as if they would never have the chance to wield them again.

By the time Beladorion got to his feet, Saeryn was upon him, beating him senseless with her steel fists. She weakened, but still she had her magic. The Beautiful Dead were strong, but they did not have the dragonborn healing. Beladorion's blood began to flow and he knew terror for the first time in his long life. He got a few good shots in, but Saeryn was a supremely skilled warrior and she mixed her hits with spells. She broke his wrist. Then his arm. She touched his chest and he began to cough up sand, but a stealthy and vicious backhand sent Saeryn reeling. Beladorion drew his blades and he and Saeryn returned to dueling. But he was, after all, physically superior and he began to move just too fast for Saeryn to follow. He cut the main artery of her leg and she fell. Were it not for her dragon blood, she would have died that very moment. Beladorion kicked her over and over again, smiling the whole time.

ASHUR HIT Andie again and by this point, she was hardly breathing. Being the highest member of the battalion, his suit wasn't affected like the others. Andie looked for Saeryn, who may have been dead already, but she couldn't see her. Her people had begun to rally against the Dead, but the weakness that had come on them all was beginning to win. By the way she witnessed her people around them slow, she knew they were affected by more than just the weariness of battle. Something was happening to them, but she didn't understand what. Some strange and powerful spell seemed to be targeting just the dragonborn, but Andie couldn't think of any such spell that could do such a thing. Her people were hardly able to stand and the Dead began to take advantage of it. They were losing.

"You're all cowards," Andie shouted, though even that proved difficult through her newfound weakness. "You wouldn't fight us when we were strong. You sneak in at the end of war, when we're tired and beginning to fade."

"I'll admit, it's not my proudest moment, but I don't care. I just want you dead, Andie. I think I always wanted you dead. I hated having to pretend I cared for you, to work with you, to be with you. Kissing you used to turn my stomach."

"Well, in hindsight, I'm not too thrilled about your face on mine either."

Ashur held his hand over her and it began to glow. Pain spread throughout Andie's body as frostbite overcame her in seconds, turning most of her body black. Ashur lowered the hand and the pain went.

"I've been practicing that one," he said. "You like? Cold seems to be sore point for your kind."

"Were you always this evil?" Andie asked, shivering.

"No. I used to be weak. Now I'm strong. Don't try to reason with me, Andie. I'm beyond your reach and your words. As a matter of fact, I'm about to take your head from your shoulders."

"Do you have any idea why you can't beat us?" she asked.

"It looks like I already have."

"No. It looks like sun."

As she said the words, the sun rose over the String Fields, high enough that its light broke into the city. As the rays hit her, Andie found her strength. She knew she couldn't lose. Not here. Not today. Ashur came in again and she drew her sword so quickly that he didn't even see it until after she'd cut him.

He cast at her and she dodged. He cast again and she countered. He drew a dagger and threw it at her, but she stopped it in midair. She still felt strangely weak, but she had figured out why. She and Ashur traded spells, but his anger was no match for her power. Her body became a humanoid flame, right down to her very core, and she became so bright he could hardly stand to look at her. She weaved around him with her blade, cutting him so fast and deep he could not keep up with her. She grabbed his arm with her flaming hand and he screamed form the pain as his flesh melted away.

"You can't beat us because you're nothing. We are the past and the future. You were never a match for me, Ashur. Or should I say *Tarven*. When we fought before I wasn't trying to kill you. I was trying to spare you. I won't make that mistake today."

"I am the commander of the—"

"You are the leader of murderers and you waited until I was weakest to face me again because somewhere, deep inside, you know you can't beat me. You were never going to win. You are a coward and a weak man. There exists no victory for people like you. You have terrified us, hunted us, and murdered us. I tried caring for you. I tried saving you. But no more. No mercy, Tarven."

She brought her other hand forward slowly, making sure it burned as hot as possible. She began to slowly push it into his chest, letting him feel every second of the pain and heat. It had been a long time coming and he has had a hand in so many atrocities, but now she was bringing him to justice, even though he could never suffer as much as he deserved. She took pleasure in the fact that he was suffering now. The shock of her white-hot hand penetrating his chest was written across his disfigured face and the last expression he wore before she turned him to a pile of smoldering Ash was one of utter confusion.

SEVERAL BLOCKS AWAY, Beladorion had completely overcome Saeryn. He had beaten her, cut her, and thrown her like a toy. Only some of her wounds healed. All around her, her people were being overwhelmed. The Dead had come upon them when they were at their absolute weakest.

"Do you know what's happening to you?" he said. "I do."

"The sun," Saeryn whispered. She gazed up at the red glow in the horizon as the sun rose and brought with it a new strength. Only, she didn't feel strengthened. Not fully. She felt confused, betrayed by her own blood. Why wasn't the sun strengthening her?

Beladorion laughed. "You're fading away, stupid Queen. You see, coming through the portal erased you from history, thus you never existed. And if you didn't exist then, you can't exist now. When I heard you and your people had returned, I began my calculations and I'm so happy to see that they were accurate to the very hour. First, you'll grow weak, then you'll simply fade away. Look to your people. It's happening now."

Saeryn rolled over and turned her head and gasped. It was true. Her people were falling. Some were even fading out of existence right before her eyes. She could hardly believe it. Beladorion took his Wrothsaield blade and plunged it into Saeryn's stomach, not a wound that would kill her instantly, but one she would not survive. She was surprised by how little it hurt. She just felt cold. But this is what it had come to. And now she knew, now she realized that there was only one way this would end. Just like Andie said.

"So, this is how we end," she said. "Fading away in the devastated streets of Arvall. I suppose that's fine with me. What's not fine is you."

She raised her broken arm toward Beladorion and froze him. Even he wasn't expecting this. Before his eyes, she snapped the bone back in place and it healed. All her wounds that weren't caused by Beladorion's blades healed. She rose, holding her bleeding stomach. She turned her wrist slowly and rose the temperature of his blood. She spread her fingers and weakened his bones.

"I have never understood one thing about your kind," she said, spitting up blood, but standing straight. "What makes you think you are a match for us? Yes, you're physically magnificent, but unless you're sneaking up on us in the forest, surprising us in a dark grotto, or descending on us when we are the weakest and most exhausted we've ever been, what makes you think any of your gifts can compare with magic?"

"You filthy traitor. I am Beladorion, leader of the—"

"The Dead? A rather appropriate name, I think. You see, all my life I've feared you, and it wasn't until today, when you and your kind snuck up on us like cowards, that I realized something. You pose no threat. You bring no danger. You are a disgrace to the dragons that gave birth to you. You are the true blood traitors."

"I will... drink... of your blood."

"You will do nothing but be what your name implies. Dead. *Eitilt mall comhlacht.*"

As she cast the time curse, the entire city froze except for the dragonborn. Saeryn limped over to Beladorion. She stared into his face.

"What is it you're so fond of saying? Oh, yes. Fhealltóir Fola."

With that she drew her sword and plunged it through his chest. She had used most of her strength and went down to her knees. She turned to address her people.

"Put them to the sword!"

The dragonborn heeded the command of their Queen and within moments the Dead were no more. Andie came rushing up to Saeryn and kneeled beside her.

"I see you took a leaf out of my book," Andie said.

"Well, they cheated. I figured we should as well." As she spoke, her people cheered. A sound so glorious yet so haunted that echoes between the crumbling structures around them. The enemy was retreating, what was left of them, and those who remained slowly perished by the hands of the fading dragonborn.

"We have to get you and our people back through the portal, Saeryn. You're fading because you've removed yourselves from the timeline. And if you all never existed, neither can I. Oh, no. What did he do to you? Oh, no, no, no..."

"We can heal me later, Andie. Let us lead our people back together."

"Some victory," Andie said.

Saeryn nodded grimly, a small smile spread across her shivering lips. "Yes. Some victory, indeed."

Saeryn called for her dragon, as did the other dragonborn. Soon they were all up and soaring through the city toward the mountain, the echoes of the songs of victory rising up in the air from the city below as the rest of the dragonborn made their way back to the University. The songs were mixed with laments of mourning, the sound eerie and haunting as they flew away from those who celebrated and wept, the rest of the city still frozen in place, unaware of the departure of their people and the dragons.

As they flew, some of the dragonborn were disappearing right from the air, their dragons, too. As they neared the foot of the mountain and began their ascent, Saeryn nearly slid from the dragon, but Andie caught her and held her tightly, trying to will her to live. They were running out of time.

They reached the University and rather than try to fit through the front doors, Andie focused her magic in one massive blast: it exploded into the mountainside, sending debris and dirt hundreds of feet in every direction. The dragonborn disappeared into the cloud.

They flew down through the clouds of dust, the exploded dirt, and entered the archives above the portal, just as the dragons and the dragonborn had first came into her time. Andie steered Ronen aside, and she kneeled down to allow her riders safely off.

Andie leapt off and inspected the portal. The portal was empty. Her heart willed with sorrow. She had to try. Andie squeezed her eyes shut and imagined the conjured image Yara had showed her in the hotel. She began whispering an incantation, almost a song, as she fought with every ounce of her being to restore the magic that Yara had shared. When she opened her eyes, she caught a trace of a glimmer. Raising her voice, Andie shouted the incantation louder, her voice echoing across the vast room. The dragonborn watched in silence as she worked her magic. Not a moment later, the portal blasted to life again, the magic within the same as she had witnessed from Yara. She smiled.

From what Yara had said, the portal was set to a time somewhere between Saeryn's and her own. Sometime after the deadly spell Saeryn's original enemy had cast to destroy all the dragonborn, and before this horrendous battle where they nearly lost to their new enemy. This was exactly what they needed.

"Oren must have found a way to calibrate the portal to this specific time when he sent Yara back," Andie whispered to herself in awe. "Yara…" Andie couldn't help but laugh. That girl had proven herself time and time again. Without her, they would have nowhere to do. She truly was a remarkable ally.

Andie grasped the smooth stone carving around the perimeter of the portal, peering into its depths. She could almost see the lush forests and waterfalls on the other side. It was a time of peace, and Oren must have somehow known it would prove useful by sending her there. Andie's heart ached at the thought of him being gone forever. She steeled herself and turned back toward her people in the room.

If she could just get the dragonborn and their dragons back to this in between time, to rejuvenate the dragon population and establish their race back into their timeline, then perhaps, just perhaps, it would stop them from fading in their current time. All they had to do was establish themselves in history, populate their people, ensure they survived until present time. Time was a dangerous thing, but it was their only hope.

"Everybody in, now!" she commanded.

There was a pause, a long moment where all the

dragonborn stared at their princess. But with a slight nod from their Queen, they moved with ferocious speed. For even the dragons began to fade, and their time was running out. The dragonborn all dove directly into the portal, some only just avoiding fading into nothing. As they were all entering, Andie hurried to Saeryn.

"Saeryn, come on, we have to get you into the portal."

"No, Andie. I'm to stay here."

"Don't be ridiculous. If you stay here, you'll die. Our people need you to lead them back to their own time and reestablish our lineage."

"No, they don't need me. They need you. You're ready, Andie. I've been grooming you since you pulled us out of the portal. I know I said I doubted you, but you have proven yourself. You have even managed to teach me."

"Saeryn no, no, no. Please don't do this. I can't go, I belong here."

"In a way you do, and in a way you never have. You're the Queen the dragonborn deserve, Andryne Rogers. You're strong, intelligent, courageous, fearless, and selfless. No one will do more or go farther for our people than you. You are the perfect Queen. Let me stay here, in the world where I finally found a bit of the peace I have searched for."

The portal began to shake and pull Andie out

across the surface. The last dragonborn entered, but the portal looked as if it was collapsing in on itself.

"It has been used too much," Saeryn said, weakly, barely able to hold her head. "It is unstable. You must go now."

"What about you?"

"I die knowing I played my part in the salvation of my people. It is as proud an accomplishment as any Queen can hope for."

"I can't lose you, Saeryn. You're the only family I have in the world. I'm begging you to live."

"This wound has ended me. And it's okay. It's perfectly okay."

Andie thought of Raesh and of all the things she'd never get to say to him. She thought of the life they would never have and the memories that she had now, but that will never be enough. She loved him. She loved Carmen and Yara. She wanted to stay and to be with her friends and enjoy the world they've fought so hard for. But that was not her destiny and she knew that.

With tears streaming down her face and the room shaking to pieces around her, Andie pulled Saeryn into her arms and held her, hoping her arms and this embrace could convey how truly thankful she was for all that Saeryn had done for her. The pain in Andie's heart was unimaginable.

A soft song rose in the room just then. A lament so

sweet and so beautiful, it brought a tear to Andie's eye. The sound came from the portal, and both dragonborn royalty turned their heads toward the haunting melody.

"They're calling to you," Saeryn smiled.

"Who are?"

"The dragons."

Andie turned down to look at her Queen. She couldn't hold back the tears. "You have been my mother, my sister, my friend, my inspiration."

"And you have been my whole world, Andie. I love you, princess."

"I love you, too, my Queen." The melody grew louder, their call more desperate as the magic of the portal wavered once more.

Andie pressed her lips to Saeryn's forehead and laid her down gently. She rose and levitated up and over the portal. She wished beyond anything that she could say goodbye to her friends, to make sure they were okay, to say goodbye to Raesh. To give him one last kiss. But they were out there somewhere, frozen in the time curse. She would have to live the rest of her days hoping that they survived. With one last look to her Queen and then up to the sky, she allowed herself to fall into the unstable surface of the portal, called by the song of the dragons.

The portal imploded just as she cleared it.

Saeryn laid on the ground, her hands and feet

numb and fading, her dragon already vanished. She was not in pain nor was she scared. She thought of Andie's face, the faces of her people, the face of her mother from so long ago. She smiled, knowing she had done her duty.

"Eitilt ar ais."

WHEN SAERYN LIFTED THE TIME CURSE, THERE WAS confusion and chaos, but the defenders of Arvall won the war and it wasn't long before reports came in from Taline that the third wave had been defeated and the portal they brought recovered. The city began the work of putting itself back together.

The Thabians and miners were sent home with commendations and the promise of aid whenever and however they should need it. The Beautiful Dead had all been killed by the dragonborn, except for Olthrion and a few others who were captured, with effort, and executed before the week was out. The Church of Stone and Sea was formally investigated, its priests imprisoned or executed as sentenced, and the Church itself demolished. The battalion was completely over; one soldier had tried to activate the icons and kill millions in a last desperate move, but Andie had deprogrammed the system months before. The politicians Ashur had bribed were rooted out and sentenced, too.

Stefan was finally able to begin rebuilding Taline in earnest. With the old University, the battalion, and the army gone, the city began to enjoy its longest peace in nearly twenty years. Yara and Bonhaus rested after the war. Some weeks later they were married and settled in Arvall. Yara and Carmen were reunited, at last. Carmen took over Marvo's restaurant, splitting her time between there and teaching at the rebuilt university, though she could never bring herself to eat the chocolate Andie brought. Lilja was never the same after losing Sarinda and Kent; she threw herself into working for the council fighters and became one of their best and most efficient.

Lymir was found unconscious, but alive beneath some rubble. When he came to some days later, he was the one who put together what happened to the dragonborn. With what he had predicted all along and the eyewitness reports of citizens who had seen the dragonborn disappear, he was able to figure out the tragic events. The news devastated millions across Noelle who had hoped the dragonborn would find peace. Lymir was broken to his core at their loss, but he put on a brave face and lead the University to the beacon of light and secured it as it always should have been.

But there was no one more broken than Raesh.

At first, Raesh couldn't bear to be around the University, so he decided to lead the council fighters in his father's stead. They went on long missions across Noelle, and even to the Old World across Shaeyara, outside the boundaries of Noelle, hunting down the last of Arvall's enemies and helping to create the safe world they deserved. When that was done, he moved to Michaelson, to Andie's old home, and commuted into Arvall every day. Lymir eventually convinced him to return to teaching and he did, becoming one of the sharpest and most beloved instructors. He never spoke of Andie, though Lymir always seemed to want to say something to him about her, as if he could somehow comfort him. Eventually, he finally submitted his books in the publishing district, only twenty blocks from his old home, and they were well received. And, after some time had passed, he finally opened his father's briefcase and joined Carmen at the restaurant.

But there was always a hole in him.

SIX YEARS PASS.

Raesh stood in Victory Garden, looking out over

the mountain Brie and down into Arvall City. It had almost finished its reconstruction, the scars from that awful war finally gone. Many things were a distant memory for him, but not those four days of horrific carnage. As he stood there, he was as content as he could be, proud to have had a hand in bringing peace to the city. It all seemed so surreal, to have finally achieved lasting peace. But it still didn't fill the void he felt in his heart. He sighed and looked up in the crimson evening sky.

There was something there. Something small and moving through the clouds. He blinked, but the thing was still there. It was moving, flying, diving toward earth, toward the mountain. He watched it descend, and, as it finally came lower, he saw what it was.

A dragon.

A dragon whose scales shone the same Byzantium hue as his beloved Andie's eyes.